A MINECRAFT MOVIE

First published in the United States by Random House Children's Books
and in Canada by Penguin Random House Canada Limited.

First published in Great Britain in 2025 by Farshore
An imprint of HarperCollins*Publishers*
1 London Bridge Street, London SE1 9GF
www.farshore.co.uk

HarperCollins*Publishers*
Macken House, 39/40 Mayor Street Upper,
Dublin 1, D01 C9W8, Ireland

Adapted by David Lewman

© 2025 Mojang AB. All Rights Reserved. Minecraft, the Minecraft logo,
the Mojang Studios logo and the Creeper logo are trademarks of
the Microsoft group of companies.

© 2025 Warner Bros. Ent. and Legendary. All Rights Reserved.

ISBN 978 0 00 869914 7
Printed in the UK

5

A CIP catalogue record for this title is available from the British Library.

All rights reserved. No part of this publication may be reproduced, stored in a retrieval system, or transmitted, in any form or by any means, electronic, mechanical, photocopying, recording or otherwise, without the prior permission of the publisher and copyright owner.

Without limiting the author's and publisher's exclusive rights, any unauthorised use of this publication to train generative artificial intelligence (AI) technologies is expressly prohibited. HarperCollins also exercise their rights under Article 4(3) of the Digital Single Market Directive 2019/790 and expressly reserve this publication from the text and data mining exception.

Stay safe online. Farshore is not responsible for content hosted by third parties.

This book contains FSC™ certified paper and other controlled
sources to ensure responsible forest management.

For more information visit: www.harpercollins.co.uk/green

THE JUNIOR NOVELIZATION

ADAPTED BY DAVID LEWMAN

CHAPTER ONE

When he was a little kid, an imaginative, adventurous boy named Steve discovered something amazing: an entrance to an abandoned mine just outside town. Who knew what thrilling adventures might await him inside? Wondrous caves! Bizarre creatures! Glittering treasures! But as he was about to enter the mine and start exploring, a scowling miner stopped him.

"Hey, kid!" the miner barked. "Can't you read?!"

He pointed to a sign: ABSOLUTELY NO CHILDREN ALLOWED!

Steve tried to dash into the mine anyway, but the miner chased him off. So instead of having exciting adventures underground, Steve did a terrible thing . . . He grew up.

At his boring grown-up job, Steve tried to find ways to be creative. He built dioramas. Wrote songs for his presentations. Wore costumes he sewed himself. But the other adults just laughed at all his efforts. *Why?* he thought. *Why can't life be more interesting? Weirder? More fun?*

As he toiled away in his drab office cubicle, Steve kept thinking about the abandoned mine he'd found in his youth. Something told him the answers he sought were down there below the surface. He had to go back and find out!

And so, thirty years after he'd first discovered the mysterious mine, Steve returned to the entrance. It was still guarded by the old miner, but this time Steve easily got past him. He jerked to the right and darted to the left, calling out, "Head fake!" He was in!

Down in the abandoned mine, Steve used a pickaxe to dig away at the sooty stone. At first he found nothing, but he wasn't discouraged. He just kept digging, until one day he unearthed a shiny crystal box and a glimmering, perfectly square cube! The two mysterious objects seemed to go together, so he put the cube inside the box.

BOOM!

A magic portal popped into view! It was a large rectangle, like a blue field glowing in a frame. Steve's eyes widened at the awesome sight. Drawn to the portal, he stepped through . . .

. . . and found himself in a strange, blocky wonderland! Everything seemed to be made out of blocks. A blocky bee buzzed by. A blocky sheep stared at Steve and said, "Baaaa!"

Steve didn't know it yet, but this bizarre realm was called the Overworld.

There was something about this place that inspired Steve, reawakening his creative impulses. He started by mining dirt blocks and stacking them into a simple house. The physics in the Overworld didn't make a lot of sense—sometimes blocks fell to the ground, and sometimes they hung in the air. But somehow it all worked perfectly for Steve. He loved building and crafting to his heart's desire. As soon as he finished his first house, he went to work on his second. Moving on from dirt blocks, he discovered he could break trees into boards and planks. In no time, Steve had built a wooden house, complete with towers and turrets!

He let his creativity run wild. Steve's third house was built out of pink sheep's wool. Sure, it burst into flames almost immediately, but for a brief moment, the fluffy house looked awesome!

To Steve, the Overworld was perfect. Except at night . . . when basically everything tried to kill him! He huddled inside his house, shaking with fear.

Zombies moaned outside, pounding on his door, while pale skeletons wandered in the dark beyond. But then one night he heard a snarl and a growl, and the moaning sounds faded. Was something scaring the creatures away?

Steve cautiously opened his front door and peeked outside. The zombies and skeletons were running away. They'd been frightened off by a big gray wolf!

"Hey—thanks, boy!" Steve told the blocky wolf gratefully. "I think you just saved my life."

The wolf turned its massive head toward Steve. Its red eyes looked menacing. It growled.

Steve held his hands up, palms out. "Whoa!" he said, trying to calm the beast down. "Easy . . . easy . . ." Looking around for something to give the wolf as a peace offering, he spotted a stray skeleton bone. He picked it up and held it out at arm's length for the wolf to take. For a moment, the wolf just stared at the bone.

Then the wolf's eyes stopped glowing red! Its mouth, full of sharp teeth, formed a smile. And a blocky collar with a name tag appeared around its neck. *POOF!*

"Atta boy," Steve said, petting him. He read the name tag. "Dennis!"

Steve and Dennis quickly became the best of

friends. Dennis loved to watch Steve chisel blocks out of the Overworld's rocky cliffs with his trusty pickaxe. He also liked to throw a blocky disk for Dennis, who would leap into the air to make the catch.

Most of all, the two pals loved to build together. When they finished a tall tower, Steve stood back with his hands on his hips, admiring their creation. "What do you think, Dennis? Should we call it the Steve-Scraper or the Steve Needle?"

"ARF!" Dennis barked.

"Yeah, buddy," Steve agreed. "Nailed it. We'll call it the Steedle."

The next day, on their morning stroll through the blocky fields and woods of the Overworld, Steve and Dennis came across some strange ruins with a shiny black obsidian gateway. One block seemed to be missing from the gateway, so Steve quickly mined a block and set it in the gap.

Dennis sniffed at a chest next to the gateway. When Steve opened the chest, he found a flint and steel inside—the tools for starting a fire. Steve struck the steel against the flint.

SHANG. SHANG. SHANK!

Sparks flew toward the doorway, and it became a swirling purple field—a portal!

Curious about where this weird gateway led, Dennis darted through.

"Dennis!" Steve cried, throwing out an arm to stop him. But it was too late.

CHAPTER TWO

Steve had no idea where the portal led. But he couldn't abandon his best friend. He took a deep breath and plunged through the glowing gateway.

Looking around, Steve didn't like what he saw.

Fire. Lava. Clouds of black smoke. And evil-looking pigs. Though he'd stepped through the portal early on a sunny morning, here it seemed to be pitch-black night. Steve had left the Overworld behind and descended into the Nether.

AROOOO!

Dennis's howl! And he sounded frightened! Steve ran to rescue his buddy. Rushing through shadowy chambers, he soon found his wolf friend in a throne room, surrounded by piglike soldiers known as piglins. Though their bodies looked basically human, their blocky heads featured piggy eyes, ears, and snouts. They were ruled by an evil piglin sorceress named Malgosha. Holding a staff, the witch turned her frightening scowl on Steve. Her face was full of selfish cruelty.

Steve stepped forward to confront the piglins and their fearsome leader. "Leave the wolf," he told them. "Take me instead."

Malgosha turned her gaze upon Steve and smiled a cruel smile. "I have a better idea. We'll take both of you. *And* that orb!"

Steve had no idea how Malgosha knew he had an object with him. He'd never thought of it as an orb, but he figured she meant the portal-summoning cube he'd found back in the abandoned mine. He quickly dug it out of his satchel, saying, "Let's get one thing straight. Where I come from, we call this a cube!"

Malgosha snatched the cube from Steve and set it atop her staff, crying, "At last! The Orb of Dominance!" She turned to her piglin guards. "Cage them!"

The piglins roughly tossed Dennis and Steve into a metal cage, slammed the door, and turned a key in the lock. *CLANG!*

Proudly wielding her staff with the Orb of Dominance on top, Malgosha immediately summoned her piglin generals. "Tomorrow," she told them, "we shall bring our Nether to the Overworld!"

The generals nodded and grunted.

Steve whispered, "We have to stop her, Dennis." The wolf stuck his blocky muzzle through the bars of the cage and slipped a set of keys off a piglin guard's belt. "Good boy, Dennis," Steve whispered, taking the keys. "Good boy!"

Later, once Malgosha and her generals had left the throne room, Steve tossed a gold bar down the hallway to distract the piglin guards, who seemed to be obsessed with gold, while he and Dennis escaped from the cage. They quickly made their way to Malgosha's chambers. Steve was able to sneak in as the piglin sorceress fed from her royal trough. *SHLURP! SHLORP!*

As Malgosha snarfed down the disgusting slop, Steve snatched the Orb of Dominance off her staff. Hearing him, the sorceress looked up from the trough, slop dripping down her hairy chin. "GUARDS!" she screamed, sending nasty bits of food flying through the air.

Steve managed to get back to Dennis before the piglin guards caught up with him. He rubbed the Orb of Dominance under his armpit and held it up to the wolf's sensitive nose. "Dennis, quick!" Steve instructed. "Take the Orb and the crystal box to Earth! Follow my scent to 149 Holly Oak Drive!"

Steve put the box and the orb into his satchel with a rolled-up note and handed it to Dennis, telling his friend, "You're this world's last hope!"

"ARF!" Dennis barked.

"No, not *avenue*!" Steve corrected. "*Drive!* Holly Oak *Drive*! Run, bud! I'll see you again. RUN!!!"

Dennis leapt out of the Nether through the glowing portal as Malgosha's piglins swarmed Steve! The brave wolf bounded across the blocky landscape of the Overworld to the Earth portal. Soon he had reached Steve's house on Holly Oak Drive in a small Idaho town. Pushing past the flap of a doggy door, Dennis found his way to Steve's room and rolled the orb and the crystal box under the bed.

Back in the Nether, Steve figured that as long as the orb stayed hidden from Malgosha, the Overworld would be safe. He just prayed some idiot wouldn't find it.

Garrett "The Garbage Man" Garrison roared down an Idaho country road in his red sports car. He was a tall guy with big muscles, thick eyebrows, long hair, and a dark beard. His car was a little worse for wear, with duct tape on the bumper. The dashboard was covered in trash and unpaid bills. But when the engine made a funny sound, Garrett just turned up the heavy-metal music blasting out of his sound system. He screeched into the parking lot of his video game store, Game Over World.

Inside, Garrett walked past the video games, the collectibles, the arcade games, and the sign reading GAMING LESSONS! 50% OFF! LEARN TO WIN LIKE A BOSS FROM THE MASTER! He paused a moment to grab a video game trophy he'd won back in 1989 and polish it on his shirt. The trophy was engraved with the words GAMER OF THE YEAR—GARRETT "THE GARBAGE MAN" GARRISON. Garrett knew those words by heart. It'd been the best year of his life.

Back in his small office, Garrett improvised breakfast, searing a steak with a blowtorch and cracking raw eggs into a glass—a meal for a bodybuilder who wanted to bulk up. He scooped some protein powder and a crushed sleeve of cookies into his mouth, but when he tried to wash it all down with a carton of milk, he found that it was empty. He coughed out a cloud of dust.

To keep his hands in shape for playing video games, Garrett squeezed a piece of grip-strengthening equipment and rotated five-pound hand weights with his wrists. Then he plunged his fingers into two cups of ice, wincing.

A short while later, Garrett played both sets of controls on an arcade game called *Hunk City Rampage,* switching back and forth between player one and player two. When he scored a bonus, he shouted, "Tell me you guys saw that!"

He was talking to three puzzled ten-year-olds—Leo, Greta, and Miles. They'd signed up for video game lessons with the ex-champ, but his "lessons" turned out to be nothing more than making his pupils watch him play.

"Why aren't you letting us play?" Leo complained.

"The male lion hunts alone," Garrett answered, working the joysticks and buttons like mad. "The children get his scraps, and they are grateful."

"But we paid you," Greta pointed out. "Aren't you supposed to be mentoring us?"

Garrett's fingers were flying. "I am. By example. Hot Garbage Tip Number One: My tutelage is best absorbed in total silence."

The three kids exchanged looks. "I think we want our money back," Greta said.

Ignoring her, Garrett kept playing even though his wrist was cramping. He played through the pain, finally beating the game's big boss. "Oooyah!" he crowed, pumping his fist. "I keep playing like this, I'll have my title back in no time." He proudly pointed to his Gamer of the Year trophy.

Leo peered at the writing on the trophy. "1989? That's all of our ages ago."

"Oh, I'm sorry," Garrett said sarcastically. "What year were *you* named world champion?"

Leo had no answer for that. Garrett grinned in triumph.

At the front door, a delivery guy asked, "Garrett Garrison?"

"No autographs today," Garrett told him, figuring the guy was a fan looking for an autograph from his hero.

Handing him a letter, the delivery guy said, "I've got your eviction notice."

CHAPTER THREE

Garrett pulled the eviction notice out of the envelope, glanced at it, and crumpled it into a ball. He looked at the three kids. "Class dismissed. See you Friday at four."

"No thanks," Miles said.

"Yeah, your mentoring program sucks," Greta said.

They laughed as they headed toward the door with no intention of coming back.

Garrett watched them go. Then he looked down at the crumpled eviction notice in his hand. He realized he was going to have to come up with the rent—or lose his store.

Garrett headed to a storage facility where the contents of abandoned sheds were put up for auction.

He knew Daryl, the guy who ran the auctions.

"Garrett the Garbage Man!" Daryl sang out when he saw him. "To what do we owe the pleasure?"

Garrett was in no mood for pleasantries. "Pleasure? You think I come to storage auctions for *fun*?" He took Daryl aside. "I'm an investor, Daryl. A businessman. I need something I can turn into cash *fast*."

Daryl grinned. "Well, you're in luck! You're gonna *love* this next storage unit! Used to be owned by some crazy miner guy. Been sitting here almost a decade."

"I'm listening," Garrett said, slightly intrigued.

Consulting a list, Daryl said, "It's got a waterbed. Some pickaxes. Turquoise-colored shirts. Just a tremendous unit."

"Really?" Garrett scoffed. "It sounds terrible!"

"And," Daryl continued, saving the best for last, "I'm pretty sure there's a 1978 Atari Cosmos."

Garrett's eyes went wide. "A Cosmos? Those things are worth a fortune."

"Heck *yeah*, they are," Daryl agreed, smiling ear to ear.

Garrett clapped a meaty hand on Daryl's shoulder. "Bro, if you can make this happen for me, I'll strongly consider hanging out with you."

"What a treat," Daryl said, rolling his eyes.

"Just keep the bidding under a hundred bucks," Garrett assured him, "and all your dreams will come true." He fist-bumped Daryl and strode off, optimistic about his prospects.

A few moments later, Daryl slammed down his gavel. "Sold! To our hometown hero Garrett 'The Garbage Man' Garrison for *nine hundred dollars*!" The other bidders wandered on to the next storage unit.

Garrett looked pale. He wasn't happy about shelling out nine hundred dollars he didn't even have . . . yet. He signed a check, ripped it from its pad, and handed it to Daryl. "I wouldn't cash this for at least six months."

Daryl stared at him in disbelief.

Inside the storage unit, Garrett quickly found the Atari Cosmos box. "Come to Papa," he said gleefully.

But when he opened the box, there was no video game console inside. Just a bunch of junk. "No," Garrett groaned. "No, no, no. Where are you?!"

He frantically tore through the contents of the unit, searching for the Cosmos. He ripped boxes open and threw the contents outside the metal shed.

Daryl ran up. "Whoa! What are you doing, man?"

Garrett wheeled on him furiously. "There's no Atari in here!"

"Well, you can't just trash the unit!"

"Not everything is about your unit, Daryl!" Garrett collapsed into a crummy folding chair. "I'm just . . . I'm up against it, man. My store. My wrists aren't what they used to be. My mentorship program is hemorrhaging students. No matter how much protein I eat, my gains are minimal. I just . . . I really needed a *win* today." He stood up and exhaled. "Wanna come hang at the shop for a bit?"

"After what I witnessed today?" Daryl asked. "No thank you. I've had enough garbage for one day." He turned and walked away.

Shaking his head, Garrett took one last look at the junk in the storage unit. Hoping for something—*anything*—of value, he dug deep, and in the back corner he found a strange cube-shaped object. When he picked it up, it glowed with a faint blue light. Hoping it might prove to be worth something, Garrett stuck it and a weird crystal box into a burlap sack and slung it over his shoulder.

While driving his sports car back to his shop, Garrett pondered his lousy life. How could things possibly get worse?

BLAM! The car's engine exploded! Black smoke billowed out from under the hood, blocking Garrett's vision. He ran his car off the road into tall grass.

CHAPTER FOUR

That same day, a young woman named Natalie and her teenage brother, Henry, drove toward their new home in Idaho. While Natalie drove, Henry drew a weird robot with pool-noodle arms in his notebook.

"Chuglass wasn't my first choice, either," Natalie was saying to Henry. "But Mom's dying wish was for us to live here . . . or at least, that's how I interpreted it."

Henry looked confused.

"Anyway," his sister continued, "the rent's super low, and I have a full-time gig. Not really a combo we can turn down right now."

"Yeah, I get it," Henry said.

"I promise you're gonna love this place," Natalie told him. "It's not just some small Idaho potato town."

Henry frowned, looking puzzled. "But that's kinda what it's known for."

He kept concentrating on his drawing. "Potato chips—"

"GAAAUUGHHH!"

Henry and Natalie were interrupted by a frustrated scream outside the car. She and Henry both stared out their windows at a car by the side of the road with a smoking engine. A man was kicking the car's bumper. They didn't know his name was Garrett . . . yet.

On the outskirts of Chuglass they passed a huge potato chip factory. Out front, a big statue of a potato chip waved at them. A sign identified the mascot as Chuggy the Chip.

"There it is," Natalie said proudly. "The famous potato chip factory."

Lowering his window, Henry asked, "What's that smell?"

"My future."

Moments later they pulled up in front of an old house—their new home. Their energetic real estate agent, Dawn Runcie, was waiting in the driveway. Natalie and Henry climbed out of the car, stiff after a long drive.

"Hi, Dawn!" Natalie called. "Nice to finally meet you."

"Hiya, Natalie!" Dawn said. "This is for you!" She

handed her a gift basket full of potato chips.

"Oh, wow," Natalie said, trying to sound impressed.

"People love working at the potato chip factory," Dawn told her.

"Yeah, I'm gonna be running their social media accounts," Natalie explained. "I promised I'd get their follower count past seventy-five."

"Nice," Dawn said, nodding. "Just take good care of your face. Everyone who works there seems to break out like crazy." She smiled at Henry. "What's up, Henry? I'm Dawn."

"Hi," Henry said. He noticed animals sticking their heads out the windows of Dawn's car, which had a ZOO ON WHEELS decal on the door. "What's up with the alpacas?" Henry asked.

"Well, real estate's not my only hustle," Dawn explained. "I also do some mobile zoo stuff on the side. Check out this new jingle I've been working on!"

She played a song on her phone, bobbing her head to the rhythm and singing along until she noticed the time. "Well, I gotta run! The mobile zoo must be on time! Madison only turns ten once. Call me if you need anything!"

"Thanks," Natalie said.

Dawn put her hand on Natalie's and lowered her voice. "Hey, I'm really sorry about your mom. It's a brave thing you're doing. Hope you know that."

In his new bedroom, Henry was unpacking books and framed pictures, trying to make the room his own. He set a photo of Natalie, himself, and their mom on a shelf. For a moment, he studied the picture, missing his mom.

Feeling sad, he reached for his notebook of drawings and ideas. Getting his brain churning always helped him shrug off sadness. As he flipped through the pages, he heard a loud noise downstairs. *CLUNK!*

"Henry!" Natalie shouted. "I could use some help down here!"

Finding the sketch of the robot he'd drawn in the car, Henry got an idea. He rummaged through moving boxes in the hall, pulling out hair dryers, pool noodles, a coffee machine, wires, and batteries.

In the kitchen, Natalie pulled a handmade pitcher shaped like a pig out of a box. Smiling, she carefully set the pig pitcher on the counter. Then she called out, "Hey! I'm not going to unpack this whole kitchen by myself! Get in here NOW!"

But instead of Henry, an odd-looking robot rolled into the room. Its base was a vacuum cleaner with hair dryers for engines blowing it forward. Its head was a coffee machine, and its arms were foam pool noodles. The whole thing seemed to be held together with red wires.

"Hi, Natalie," the robot said in a high-pitched monotone. "I've heard a lot—lot—lot—lot—lot about you!" A few sparks flew off the robot. Henry followed it into the kitchen.

"Henry, what is this?" Natalie asked.

"He's our new Buddy Bot," he explained. "He can help us around the house."

"Here's a coffee while I vacuum," the robot chirped, "so you can re-re-re-relax!"

More sparks burst out of the robot's neck. Natalie frowned.

"He's fine," Henry reassured her. "Don't worry about it."

"I've got a big day tomorrow, and this isn't helping," Natalie said.

"Sorry," said Henry. "I was just trying to have a little fun."

"I know," Natalie said, trying to be patient with her little brother. "It's just, every time you do, you ruin our stuff. Can you just try to act a little more . . . normal?"

"I *am* normal," Henry said, offended.

The Buddy Bot sparked again. Rolling around and flailing its pool-noodle arms, it knocked the pig pitcher off the counter. *SMASH!*

Natalie stared at the pieces on the floor, horrified. "Henry! Mom made that for me!"

"Oh my gosh," Henry said, equally horrified. "I'm so sorry—"

"Uh-oh!" the robot squeaked. "I'm the m-m-m-messy roommate!"

Natalie started picking up the broken shards of pig. "I don't think this crap is cute like Mom did. So grow up already!"

CHAPTER FIVE

The next morning when Henry came into the kitchen, Natalie was pulling a baking sheet out of the oven. "Hey," she said gently. "I didn't mean to snap last night. I'm just really stressed."

"It's okay," Henry said.

"Check it out," Natalie said, holding up the baking sheet. "I made you Mom's famous tater-tot breakfast pizza. So you can hand out slices on your first day."

Henry looked puzzled. "I thought you wanted me to seem 'normal.' And now you want me to bribe people with slices of breakfast pizza?"

"And," Natalie continued enthusiastically, ignoring her brother's question, "I did a little digging online. Signature scents for young men are huge here." She handed him a canister. "So I got you some body spray."

Henry read the label. "'Velvet Mischief'?"

"You wanna spray it and then walk into it," she instructed. "Don't be too direct. It's very powerful."

Henry grabbed his backpack.

"Hey," Natalie said. "I love you."

"Love you too," Henry said. He sprayed the Velvet Mischief and walked through it on his way out.

Natalie waved her hand. "Whew. That *is* powerful."

On his way to school with the tray of breakfast pizza carefully balanced on the handlebars of his bike, Henry noticed the Game Over World video game store. Just his kind of place! He checked his watch, saw he had a few minutes to spare, and headed in, carrying the tater-tot pizza.

He looked at all the video games and collectibles. Then he noticed a cube sitting in a chest. Feeling strangely drawn to the curious object, he reached toward it—

"Yo!" Garrett barked. "Not open yet!" He was still sorting through boxes from the storage unit.

"Sorry," said Henry. "Your store is really cool."

"I know," Garrett said immodestly. "Looking for anything in particular?"

Henry shook his head. "No, just checking stuff out."

"Noncommittal," Garrett observed. "Classic loser

mentality. I can help with that." He handed Henry a flyer that read *Mentoring by Garrett "The Garbage Man" Garrison: Trash your old life and start winning!* "I'm starting a mentorship program for people who want to win at the game of life. Fifty bucks an hour."

"Cool," Henry said uncertainly, reading the flyer. "How do you actually 'win' at life?"

Garrett smiled. "Nice try. That is literally the answer I charge money for." He noticed the tray Henry was holding. "What's with the breakfast pizza?"

"Oh, my sister made it," Henry explained. "I'm supposed to hand out slices at school to make friends."

Garrett winced. "Ouch." Then he sniffed. "I notice you're also wearing Velvet Mischief. It's a great cologne, and I strongly believe every young man should have a signature scent. But it may not be right for you."

Henry turned his head toward his shoulder and smelled himself. "I didn't think I applied very much."

"No one ever does," Garrett replied. "Listen, I'm gonna give you a free Hot Garbage Tip: Friendship is like a puzzle. Sometimes you think it needs to have a lot of pieces to be cool. And sometimes just one piece is cool, and then people will say, 'That's not a puzzle. That's just a picture.' And they've got a right to speak, too." He sat on the edge of his desk. "Any questions?"

"Yes," Henry said, looking baffled. "Quite a few."

"My point is," Garrett said, "there's no *I* in *team*. But there are two in *winning*."

"Okay," Henry said, sticking the flyer in his satchel. "Well, I gotta go to school."

"Okay, nerd," Garrett said. "Just trust me—leave the pizza."

One of Henry's first classes was art, taught by Mr. Gunchie, who wore shorts, a turtleneck, and a whistle around his neck. "All right, class," Mr. Gunchie announced after the bell rang, "let's all say hi to Henry. This is his first day in a new school. So one, two, three, 'Hi, Henry.'"

None of the students said anything. A couple of them coughed.

"Hi," Henry said, finding a seat.

"All right, I'm Mr. Gunchie," the teacher continued. "For those of you who don't know me, I teach gym, but now, thanks to budget cuts, I also teach art." He turned to the new student. "Okay, we're gonna shoot you right out of the cannon, Henry. Today we're drawing a still life." He plopped two pieces of fruit on a plate. "One orange, one banana. Let's get after it, people!" He blew his whistle. *TWEEEET!*

The students started drawing. Henry sketched feverishly, getting into it. Mr. Gunchie paced around the room. After a while, he blew a short blast on his whistle. *TWEET!*

"Okay, eyes up front." He picked up a drawing by a kid named Trevor and held it so everyone could see. "Everyone have a look at this. Just incredible. I feel like I'm there. Trevor, what color would you say you mostly landed on for the orange?"

Trevor shrugged. "Just your basic orange, I guess."

"Don't get discouraged, kids," Mr. Gunchie said. "We can't all be Trevor. It would be a mistake to try." He tossed the orange to Trevor. Then he resumed walking around the room inspecting the pupils' drawings.

When he got to Henry, he stopped.

"Uh-oh," Mr. Gunchie said, making a *T* with his hands. "Time out, time out." He snatched Henry's sketchbook and showed his drawing to the class. It showed a banana with a detailed jet pack strapped on its back. "This is not the assignment," Mr. Gunchie told Henry accusingly. "Don't you know what a still life is? It means you just draw the thing."

"Well, I had an idea and kinda got excited," Henry enthused. "It's a jet pack design I've been working on—"

"Not very *realistic,* is it?" Mr. Gunchie interrupted, snapping Henry's sketchbook shut.

"Neither was Dalí's," Henry said, referring to the surrealist painter Salvador Dalí. He figured any art teacher would know about Salvador Dalí.

He figured wrong.

"Well, I went to Dollywood on my honeymoon," Mr. Gunchie said, fondly remembering his trip to Dolly Parton's theme park, "and I don't recall seeing any flying bananas. Let's try again." He blew a few short blasts on his whistle. *TWEET! TWEET! TWEET!* Then he tossed Henry a pink eraser and walked back to his desk at the front of the classroom.

Trevor leaned over to Henry. "That jet pack would never work."

"Well, if you calculate thrust to mass, it's kinda foolproof, actually," Henry insisted. "It's just math."

A friend of Trevor's leaned in. "My dad says math's been debunked."

"Check it out," Trevor taunted. "New kid thinks he's a rocket scientist."

Henry didn't see how this could possibly be an

insult. "I would *love* to be a rocket scientist."

"Okay," Trevor said. "So prove it."

Henry got a glint in his eye.

CHAPTER SIX

Later that day, Mr. Gunchie, Trevor, and some other students gathered around Henry on the football field. He was putting the jet pack he'd secretly assembled in science class onto a skeleton he'd borrowed from the lab.

As Henry checked his calculations in his notebook, one of Trevor's buddies stealthily cut a wire on the jet pack.

"All right," Henry said, satisfied with his final calculations. "Count us down, Trevor."

"Five . . . four . . . three . . . ," Trevor and the other students chanted.

BWOOOOSH! The skeleton blasted off early. It spiraled into the distance, heading straight toward the Chuggy Potato Chip factory!

The other kids and Mr. Gunchie ran off. "I was never here, all right?" Mr. Gunchie yelled as he ran. But Henry just stood there, unable to look away.

BOOM! The jet-packed skeleton crashed into a smokestack, knocking it into the Chuggy the Chip statue. The smokestack and the beloved mascot both fell into the river below the factory. *SPLOOOOOSH!*

Henry was immediately summoned to the vice principal's office. She told him, "The good news is no one died. The bad news is you've disrupted the supply chain for potato chips all across America."

"I'm so sorry," Henry apologized. "It was an accident."

"This could be grounds for expulsion, Henry," the vice principal warned him. "I need you to call your guardian."

In the hallway outside the vice principal's office, Henry brought up Natalie's number on his phone. He stared at it for a second, knowing she'd be upset and furious. So instead, he called a different number. . . .

"Game Over World," Garrett answered.

"Uh, Mr. Garbage Man?" Henry said quietly, looking around to make sure no one was listening. "It's Henry. The kid with the tater-tot breakfast pizza."

"Ohhhh, right," Garrett said, remembering. "Look, the flavors were there, but when you cover the tots like that, they get all steamed—"

"Sorry," Henry interrupted, eager to get to the

point. "Hey, um, I have a weird favor to ask. Can you come to my school and pretend to be my uncle?"

"What?" Garrett said, surprised. "No way, man."

Henry checked his pockets. "I have . . . twenty-six bucks."

Garrett's car roared up to the school moments later. The vice principal was waiting outside with Henry. Garrett jumped out of the car and said, "Hi. I'm Henry's uncle."

"You?" the vice principal asked. "The Trash Bag?"

"Garbage Man," Garrett corrected, smiling his most charming smile.

She bought it.

Garrett took Henry back to Game Over World with him. "So what's the deal, kid?" Garrett asked as they walked into the shop.

"Well, you hear what happened at the potato chip factory today?" Henry asked.

Garrett nodded. The news was all over town.

"That was me," Henry admitted.

"Whoa, that was you?" Garrett asked. "You going to juvie or something?" He guessed anyone who knocked over the town mascot was bound to end up in a juvenile detention facility.

Henry looked miserable. "I don't know. I don't know what's going to happen. But I probably just cost my sister her job."

Henry opened his satchel. The flyer that Garrett had given him earlier was stuck between the pages of his sketchbook. When he pulled it out, the book opened, displaying one of his drawings. Curious, Garrett picked it up and flipped through its pages. "This stuff ain't bad, kid," he said, impressed by Henry's drawings. "First banana in space? I dig it. Maybe I'm not the only true talent in Chuglass."

"Well," Henry said, "the entire world would disagree with you." He grabbed the sketchbook out of Garrett's hands, snapped it shut, and tossed it in the trash.

Garrett winced. The kid really *was* having a bad day.

But then something in the store caught Henry's eye: a cube in a burlap sack.

It was glowing!

CHAPTER SEVEN

"Whoa!" Henry said, moving toward the sack. "What's this?"

Garrett looked to see what he was talking about. "No idea," he admitted. "Probably some New Age junk. I could let it go for around nine hundred bucks."

Henry opened the sack. The cube, lying next to the crystal box, glowed brighter. "I wonder what it does," he murmured.

The cube's blue light started to pulsate in sync with Henry's heartbeat. He stared at the hypnotizing object. Finally, he lifted the cube. Underneath, he spotted a worn sheet of paper with writing scrawled on it.

"Wait, there's instructions," Henry said. "'Never under any circumstances combine the Orb and Earth Crystal box,'" he read.

Garrett walked up behind him, entranced by the

glowing cube. "Here's one more fresh Hot Garbage Tip. On the house," he said. "Winners don't follow instructions!"

Henry nervously took a breath and placed the orb in the crystal box. *SHOOOOM!* The combination of orb and box started pulling him toward the door. "It feels like it wants to *go* somewhere!" he exclaimed.

Garrett flipped the sheet of paper over, finding more writing. "Wait," he said. "You didn't read everything. 'Do not follow this orb! Even if you're a struggling business owner and need a ton of cash fast . . . because *there's loads of treasure down here. But it's not worth the danger!*' " He looked at Henry with his eyes shining.

Treasure! He could save his store!

Henry shook his head. "I *can't*, man. Natalie will kill me. I've already caused enough trouble for one lifetime."

Still pulsing with blue light, the orb shook in its crystal box.

With a few of her petting zoo animals riding along in her car, Dawn the real estate agent pulled into Natalie and Henry's driveway, responding to

Natalie's frantic phone call.

"Sorry!" Natalie called, running out the front door. "I tried everything. I didn't know who else to call."

"All good!" Dawn assured her. "What's going on?"

"I can't find Henry. I tried the school. I tried his phone a million times. He should have been home hours ago."

"I would have thought he'd still be in detention for killing Chuggy."

"What?!" Natalie cried. "That was *him*?"

"Gimme your phone," Dawn ordered.

"Oh my gosh," Natalie said, handing Dawn her phone. "I can't believe this. We're here for one day and already Henry's the town villain."

Dawn used the Find My Phone feature on Natalie's phone to locate Henry. "Got him. He's fine. He's just playing in a mineshaft."

"WHAT?!"

Dawn headed toward her car. "Hop in. I'll drive." She handed Natalie a bag and nodded toward a llama in the back seat. "Here—you can feed Mr. Scribbles some of these busted carrots. And I'd do it now if you enjoy having a face."

"I really don't mind driving myself," Natalie said.

The pulsing cube had led Henry and Garrett to the abandoned mine discovered by Steve years before. A rusty sign warned DANGER! NO TRESPASSING BY LAW!

"Forget it," Henry said when he saw the sign. "Let's go home."

"We can't turn back now," Garrett insisted. "We've come too far."

"It's only been like seven minutes," Henry pointed out.

"Stand back, Hank," Garrett said. He grabbed the rusty chain on the gate and tried to break it. As he struggled, grunting and straining, Henry flicked the latch on the gate and walked through. "Very good, Hank," Garrett said, covering. "You pass the test that I planned for you some time ago."

They entered the shadowy mine. The glowing cube lit their way as they walked past collapsed timbers.

"Look!" Henry said, pointing ahead.

Deep in the mine tunnel, the frame of a mystical portal glowed blue in the darkness. As they approached the shimmering portal, the cube in Henry's hand glowed even brighter.

"Looks like a treasure wind to me," Garrett said slowly, amazed by the sight of the portal.

"Henry! What are you doing here?!" Natalie cried, rushing up behind them with Dawn. Henry and Garrett both jumped, startled. Natalie pointed her thumb at Garrett. "Who is this guy?"

"He's my new mentor," Henry gasped, still recovering from the surprise.

"Hey," Garrett said, smiling and raising a hand. "I'm Garrett the Garbage Man."

"Sorry, what?" Natalie asked.

"Hey, guys!" Henry cried. He was being pulled toward the portal by the cube!

Garrett grabbed hold of Henry, but the cube's pull was too strong, even for a big guy like him. Natalie grabbed Garrett, and Dawn grabbed Natalie, but Henry was still being drawn into the opening.

"Henry!" Natalie yelled. "Let go of that thing!"

Henry looked at the cube. Sure, he could just let go. Do the safe thing. The normal thing.

But he didn't.

Instead, Henry closed his eyes and let the portal pull him through, along with Garrett, Natalie, and Dawn.

CHAPTER EIGHT

SHWOOMP! WHUMP!

Henry shot out of the other end of the portal and tumbled onto the grass of the Overworld. The orb and the crystal box flew out of his hands and landed on the ground.

Lying there, Henry felt the blades of grass between his fingers. They definitely felt weird—not like grass back home. Could they possibly be . . . *square?* He sat up and looked around at the bizarre blocky landscape.

WHUMP! WHUMP! WHUMP!

Garrett, Natalie, and Dawn came flying out of the portal, landing on Henry in a big pile. Groaning, they untangled themselves, stood up, and stared at the place they found themselves in.

It was quite a sight.

Everything looked cubic. The mountains looked like sets of stairs. Chunky clouds floated over them.

A square sun shone in the sky.

Scanning the countryside all the way to the horizon, they saw desert, jungle, tundra, plains, and an ocean in the distance. None of it looked normal.

"We're not in Idaho anymore," Garrett muttered, amazed.

Natalie shook her head and rubbed her eyes, refusing to believe they were seeing anything real. "I think we're experiencing a shared delusion. Group insanity. The French call it a folie à deux."

Garrett snorted. "The French have some stupid word for everything."

"That's just called language," Dawn pointed out. "Who are you, again?"

"Garrett 'The Garbage Man' Garrison. Gamer of the Year, 1989."

Henry picked up the cube. Pulsating in his hand, it began to pull him again. "Garrett," he said, "this orb still wants to go somewhere. It's pulling me toward that weird pink thing over there."

Garrett looked to see what Henry was referring to. When he saw a pink sheep, his gamer's instinct kicked in. "Hm, a local beast," he said knowingly. "If this is what I think it is, that's our first quest giver." He grinned. "Hank, we're gonna be rolling in riches very soon! I'll do the talking."

Henry and Garrett hurried toward the pink sheep, tugged by the pulsating orb.

"Henry!" Natalie called to her brother. "Get back here!" She and Dawn ran after the two treasure hunters.

Deep in the gloomy Nether, piglins pounded gold into armor and weapons. The only craftwork permitted there was making things for war and destruction. Or for the glory and honor of their leader.

Malgosha smiled a sickening grin as she watched the top of her staff flicker and spark back to life. "The Orb of Dominance!" she hissed, her eyes flashing with desire. "It has returned!" She remembered how the Orb had been stolen from her so many years ago. And who had stolen it . . .

Flanked by two guards, Malgosha went straight to the dungeon where Steve was still being held prisoner. He was filthy, with tangles in his long beard and his hands chained to the rock wall. Despite the chains, he was chiseling a statue of the piglin sorceress. When he saw her, he dropped his chisel.

"Malgosha! My liege!" he cried. "Super stoked you're here. Would you like some glad tidings? In the form of a song I've written in your honor?" He started to hum.

Malgosha slammed the base of her staff on the stone floor.

BAMMMM!

"I'll take that as a no," Steve said.

"The Orb has returned!" she announced.

Steve's eyes widened. "It can't be. Has Dennis brought it?"

"With the Orb's power, I'll block out the sun and destroy the Overworld once and for all!" She cackled. "You stole the Orb from me," she said, pointing her staff at Steve's chest, "and now you will retrieve it."

As best he could with his hands chained to the wall, Steve bowed. "It would be a privilege, my liege!"

"We're going to unbind you now," Malgosha continued, nodding to her guards. "Don't do anything foolish."

"Of course not," Steve replied. But as soon as the piglins had freed his hands, Steve grabbed one of the guard's blades and held it to Malgosha's throat, shouting, "SNEAK ATTACK!"

Laughing, Malgosha held up Dennis's collar. "Go

ahead," she dared him. "Strike me down. My piglins will make a meal of your beloved wolf."

"Dennis?" Steve asked. "Where is he? How do I know you're telling the truth?"

"You don't," Malgosha said. "There's only one way to find out. The Orb . . . for your little dog's *life*."

CHAPTER NINE

Garrett, Henry, Natalie, and Dawn gathered around the pink sheep, which was contentedly munching on grass, ignoring them.

Garrett stepped forward and spoke slowly. "Hello, wise quest giver. We humbly seek gold. Give us a quest that will lead us to your treasure load."

The pink sheep just kept eating.

"Garbage Man," Dawn said, "I work in the animal field, and I am telling you that thing doesn't understand a word you're saying."

Natalie gestured toward the cube in Henry's hands. "What is that thing? Why are we following it?

"Because it's gonna lead us to treasure," Henry explained.

"You seriously *believe* that?" Natalie asked.

"Uh, yeah," Garrett said confidently. "Hank's holding the treasure magnet! We're about to be gazillionaires." He rubbed his hands together greedily.

"This is not how you solve problems in real life," Natalie said. "With magic cubes." She started to walk off and said firmly, "C'mon, Henry. Let's go."

"Yeah," Dawn agreed, following her. "I gotta get home and make a cheese board for a quinceañera," she explained.

Suddenly, the sky shifted from day to night. A cubic moon replaced the sun. A wolf howled. *AROOOO!*

"Great," Natalie said. "Now it's dark."

"Did that sunset feel real quick to anyone else?" Dawn asked.

The wolf's howl was soon followed by other disturbing sounds: gurgling, hissing, growling, and moaning. The noises seemed to be coming from the dark woods nearby. Frightened, the pink sheep ran off.

"Guys," Henry asked nervously, "what's happening?"

Shapes were moving in the darkness.

"All right, everyone stay calm," Garrett said. "Free Hot Garbage Tip: Fear is just weakness taking control of your body's cockpit. And if that happens, you can say goodbye to your body plane's navigation system."

"What?" Natalie asked, utterly confused by Garrett's advice.

Skeletons burst out of the woods! Armed with bows, they shot arrows as they charged forward! Henry, Natalie, and Dawn screamed. Garrett took off running. The others ran in a different direction toward a stand of trees.

As Malgosha looked on, piglin guards escorted Steve to the portal between the Nether and the Overworld. The portal shimmered with sickly purple energy.

"Find the Orb!" Malgosha commanded. "You have three poop cycles to complete this task."

Steve made a face. "I think you mean three *days*." Shaking his head, he stepped toward the portal. "Gosh, you people are *disgusting*."

Garrett kept running, arrows whizzing by his head. Looking ahead, he saw another horde of skeletons, who immediately started chasing him. "AAAAHHH!" Garrett screamed.

Not watching where he was going, Garrett fell into a deep hole. *WHUMPF!* A cloud of dirt rose from the pit.

At the bottom of the hole, Garrett winced with pain and pulled a pickaxe from underneath his butt. When he looked up, he saw skeletons staring down at him from the rim, fitting arrows to their bows.

"Aw, no!" Garrett groaned. Out of desperation, he swung the pickaxe at the wall of dirt in front of him. Blocks of dirt disappeared! Without really understanding how this was possible, Garrett swung his pickaxe again and again, tunneling horizontally away from the hole before arrows rained down on him.

At the same time, Henry, Natalie, and Dawn ran through the woods. Cube-headed skeletons riding red-eyed spiders—spider jockeys—were closing in on them from all sides. "Run!" Natalie shouted.

The spider jockeys fired their arrows, but instead of hitting their targets, they accidentally shot each other. They began to fight among themselves. In the confusion, Henry, Natalie, and Dawn escaped into a clearing. Henry glanced back to see if they were being pursued. When he turned to look where he was going, he ran right into a tree. *WHAM!*

The orb and crystal box flew out of his satchel, landing in a pile of leaves.

Natalie ran over to Henry. "Hey, are you okay?"

Henry was staring at the tree he'd run into. The

part of the trunk he'd smacked into had disappeared! The top half of the tree was floating, supported by nothing. Henry waved his hand through the space between the stump and the upper half. It seemed . . . impossible!

"Whoa . . . ," Henry said.

Natalie stared, too. "This can't be happening. Trees don't float."

"Trees in *our* world don't float," Henry corrected her. He felt around the tree, thinking. Then he punched the trunk. Another cubic chunk flew out. He punched again, fascinated.

They heard gurgling sounds. They all turned to see what was making them.

"Gang," Dawn said, "we got a zombie problem."

CHAPTER TEN

The zombies were lurching toward them. Luckily, zombies are slow.

Henry picked up a cubic chunk. Instinctively, he half threw and half placed it. As he did so, it expanded into a large wooden block! He tossed more cubes, and they all turned into wooden blocks.

"Henry," Natalie snapped impatiently, "we don't have time to play around with blocks right now! We're about to die!"

Henry stacked several of the blocks into a wall and kicked it. It held. The wall was solid! "Nat, I think I can *help*," Henry said. "Just let me."

"Fine!" Natalie said, amazed by the wall Henry had built. She saw the zombies staggering toward them. "Just do it! Do it! Do it!"

Henry leapt into action, knocking cubes out of trees, turning them into blocks, and building a structure for them to take refuge in. The structure grew quickly. Henry's improvised plan was working!

Unfortunately, though, he'd forgotten that he'd left the orb and crystal box in the leaves *outside* the structure. . . .

Once Garrett figured he'd tunneled far enough away from the pit surrounded by skeletons, he started digging up toward the surface. Soon his head popped out into the fresh air. He inhaled deeply, glad to be aboveground again.

Scanning the area, Garrett spotted patrolling spider jockeys. He stayed perfectly still until the coast was clear. While he was frozen, something snuck up behind him—a green creature with a square head, a rectangular body, and four cubelike feet, two in front and two in back.

Sensing something behind him, Garrett whipped around, startled, and punched the creature in the face without thinking. The green thing looked stunned.

"Oh my gosh," Garrett apologized. "Dude. I'm so sorry."

A light inside the creeper began to pulsate, accompanied by a hissing sound.

"You trying to tell me something, little fella?"

Garrett asked. "I didn't mean to punch you. You just totally creeped up on me—"

BOOOOOM!

The creeper exploded, blowing Garrett sky-high! He fell to the ground, landing hard. *WHUMP!* When he looked up, he saw spider jockeys coming his way. He also spotted Henry's cubic shelter in an open field.

"Garrett!" Henry called from the top of the tower. "Over here!"

Garrett ran, pursued by skeletons and zombies. As he headed toward the shelter, he spied the orb and crystal box lying in the leaves and scooped them up.

"Garrett! Hurry!" Henry shouted.

As Garrett sprinted toward the tower, an arrow knocked the orb and crystal box from his hands! The box hit the ground and shattered into fragments. Without the crystal box, they'd never be able to open the portal to their own world again!

Garrett picked up the orb and box fragments and ran to the shelter, pounding on its wall. "Help! Help!"

Zombies reached him. He knocked them away, but they kept coming back. "Hank!" he screamed. "Open the door!"

From atop the structure's roof, Henry peered over

the edge at Garrett. "There is no door! Hold on, I'm coming!"

"Henry!" Natalie warned. Her brother turned and saw a zombie coming up the stairs to the roof. "I thought you sealed this place up."

"I did!" Henry insisted. "It's like it appeared out of nowhere." He, Natalie, and Dawn crouched, backing away from the zombie.

Below, Garrett was doing his best to fight the horde of zombies that kept attacking him. There seemed to be an endless supply of the ghoulish fighters.

On the roof, Henry sidestepped the zombie and kicked it from behind, knocking it off the edge. It plummeted to the ground, landing face-down next to Garrett. Slowly, it returned to life.

As another zombie tried to bite Garrett, Henry knocked out blocks from the inside of the shelter, yanked Garrett in through the hole, and sealed it back up. Inside, the two of them stood there for a moment, breathing hard.

"Garrett," Henry asked, "why'd you leave us?"

"Sorry, kid," Garrett said, affectionally slapping him on the arm. "Dead dudes can't win Gamer of the Year."

Henry looked confused and a little hurt.

Outside, a creeper blew a hole in the shelter. *BOOOOM!* Zombies and skeletons rushed in. Garrett and Henry ran up the stairs.

On the roof, Henry, Natalie, Dawn, and Garrett huddled together, trapped. "Guys," Garrett said, "if I don't make it, tell my story in song. A heavy-metal song. Long. With chapters."

"To think we're all going to die," Dawn said sadly. "I had things I wanted to do."

Natalie held Henry close. "I had one job: Keep you alive. And I blew it."

"This isn't your fault," Henry assured her. She hugged him tight.

Then they heard something. . . .

CLANK. CLANK. CLANK.

CHAPTER ELEVEN

Everyone—the zombies, the skeletons, and the humans—turned toward the sound.

Though Henry, Garrett, Natalie, and Dawn didn't know it yet, it was Steve, tapping his sword against the rooftop's ledge. "Hey, night jerks," he said. "Remember me? Let's dance!"

Steve charged into battle, snapping a zombie's neck. "Go to sleeeeeep!" he told it. He head-butted another zombie and shoved him off the shelter. Spinning and swinging his sword, Steve mowed down monster after monster with incredible moves. Henry was amazed by the stranger's fighting skills.

The sun rose, and the remaining fiends burst into flame. Steve knocked down one last dying skeleton with his elbow. "Kill shot!"

"Lame," Garrett scoffed. "Guy was dead anyway."

"Whoa," Henry said. "Who are you?"

"I," Steve announced dramatically, "am Steve."

It was clear that the other four humans had all been expecting a grander answer. Something that started with *Sir* or *Master* or even *Super.*

"Who are you people?" Steve asked in turn. "Where's Dennis?"

Henry looked puzzled. "We don't know any Dennis."

"Then how'd you get *that*?" Steve asked, reaching for the cube in Garrett's hand.

Garrett held the cube out of reach. "Easy, homeslice!" he warned. "This is *my* property. I overpaid for it. Quite drastically."

"Do you even know what that is?" Steve challenged, pointing at the blocky object. "That's the Orb of Dominance!"

"That's a cube," Natalie told him.

Steve shook his head. "You people seriously have no idea what you're dealing with. Give the Orb to me and no one gets hurt."

"No way," Natalie countered. "We need it to get home."

The broken box was in Garrett's other hand. Steve peered at it. "Broken?! Hate to take a big fat dumper-roo on your plans, but without the Earth Crystal box, you *can't* get home!"

"Garbage Man busted it," Dawn said accusingly.

"Nah-uh," Garrett said.

While Garrett was concentrating on the broken box, Dawn swiped the Orb and handed it to Henry. "Why don't you hold this, Henry? Pure of heart and all that." Henry stashed the Orb in his satchel.

"Hey, so do I," Garrett protested.

Looking worried, Natalie took a step toward Steve. "Are you implying that we're stuck here?"

"No," Steve answered, "I'm just saying it flat out. There is only *one* way you could ever replace that broken Earth Crystal box. In the Woodland Mansion. But going there would get you all killed."

"So would staying here," Henry said, thinking of the zombies and skeletons that came out at night.

"Fair enough," Steve conceded. He thought a moment. "Listen, I can get you back home. But then you gotta give me the Orb. I made a deal to retrieve it for a piglin queen."

"What are you going to do with it?" Henry asked.

"That's none of your concern," Steve told him. "But let's just say I have a double cross in mind. So a temporary alliance. What do you say? Do we have a deal?"

The four looked at each other.

Henry nodded to Natalie and Garrett. "He did just waste, like, twenty creatures. So maybe we join forces. For the time being."

"It was more like seventeen," Garrett objected. "But okay. Under two conditions." He turned and faced Steve. "One: Always address *me*, because I'm the *leader*. Two: If you double-cross us, I'll crack your head between my butt cheeks like a *walnut*."

"I'm so sorry," Dawn apologized to Steve. "We just met this man."

"Well, Dr. Swollenstein here just got himself a deal," Steve said, shaking hands with Garrett. "All right. First we need to load up on some gear or we're all gonna die. Let's head to Midport Village!" He started off.

Henry followed him. "Um, Mr. Steve? How did you *do* any of that?"

Garrett didn't love seeing Henry so impressed by Steve.

Down in the eternal night of the Nether, Malgosha sat on her throne awaiting news of the Orb of Dominance. A piglin messenger got close to her ear, then oinked loudly. *OINK!*

Malgosha pulled away from the messenger. "If you're not going to whisper, then stand over there!"

The messenger backed off and resumed oinking.

"The Orb is with four Roundlings?" Malgosha translated, using their term for humans. "So Steve betrays me. As foreseen. He's certain to take them to Midport Village. It will be the last place any of them draws breath. General Chungus! Step forward."

A huge, terrifying piglin officer stepped out of the shadows. The other piglins cowered as he passed by. But when he opened his cruel mouth, he spoke in a surprisingly high-pitched and gentle voice. "Yes, Your Highness?"

"Take your finest warriors and bring me the Orb," Malgosha commanded. "This time, kill the Roundlings."

"Sure, no problem," General Chungus squeaked, nodding. "Even Steve?"

"Especially Steve!" Malgosha hissed.

"Aw, that's too bad," Chungus said, disappointed. "I kinda like that guy. Knows how to throw a mean dungeon party. Has great energy."

Malgosha handed him a glowing red vial. "Here. Take this Nether wart so you don't zombify. This is all I have." Without drinking Nether wart, the piglins would turn into zombies under the bright Overworld sun.

"Thanks heaps, Malgosha," Chungus said,

holding up the vial. "But I don't think this is gonna be enough. Last time we lost a lot of good piglins up there."

"Make it work!" Malgosha snarled.

"All right." Chungus shrugged. "We'll be on our way, then." He passed the vial to his piglin troops, who chugged Nether wart from it. "Drink up, boys. You don't wanna zombify up there. Overworld kinda stinks for us piglins."

They headed through the portal, bound for the Overworld.

CHAPTER TWELVE

Steve led Henry, Natalie, Dawn, and Garrett into a beautiful, busy town. The sun shone on timber-framed buildings. Mountains rose in the distance. A huge stone arch served as a natural entryway. "Here it is," Steve announced. "Midport Village. I've got a secret stash of elite loot that'll help us survive the Woodland Mansion."

Dawn noticed cubic citizens with long noses curiously staring at them as they walked through the streets. "Hold up," she said. "Who are these guys?"

"Oh, these dudes?" Steve asked. "They're the villagers!"

"They're not going to eat us, right?" Natalie asked.

"No!" Steve chuckled. "Of course not. They're total pacifists. And vegetarians. You don't bug them, they won't bug you. They just like to trade, chill out, and eat buttloads of bread. They love crushin' loaf." He gestured toward a villager who was biting into a long loaf of brown bread at that very moment. "But it's actually a pretty sweet community. Each villager plays an important role. Except the nitwit. Each village gets one. Kind of a town idiot. But we like 'em."

Steve nodded toward a villager repeatedly walking into a shut door. *BONK. BONK.* A cow watched the nitwit, slowly chewing its cud.

"So the villagers built all this?" Garrett said, looking up at the homes and shops.

"Yep," Steve confirmed. "You know what's even crazier? I've never even seen them use their hands! It's insane!"

They passed a very tall ladder leading to a diving board. Llamas were lined up, waiting to jump off the board. One bounced off and landed in a tiny pool. *SPLASH!*

"What's that?!" Henry asked.

Steve looked over casually to see what Henry was asking about. "The world's tallest diving board going into the world's smallest pool. I built that years ago."

Another llama bounced off the diving board and plunged into the pool. *SPLASH!*

"Looks like you got yourself a llama problem," Garrett observed. "This is what happens with no alpha present." He resented being led around by Steve and didn't want to miss an opportunity to criticize him.

But Dawn was impressed by the diving llamas. "Wow," she gushed, "they're incredible!"

"And you built it?" Henry asked.

"Yes, and tons of other stuff!" Steve said proudly.

As if on cue, a pig with a crown walked by.

"Whoa," Henry said, transfixed by the creature. "Is that . . . some kinda king?"

"No," Steve said. "That's a legend." He watched Henry's face light up with joy. "Whatever you can dream here, you can make. Zero limits! You know what I'm talking about. That was your shelter, right? Pretty killer for a first build."

That made Henry feel good. Back in Idaho, people didn't seem to appreciate his creations very often.

"Look out!" Natalie cried. A big gray metallic figure covered in yellow-flowered green vines lumbered by. It resembled a robot with arms that reached almost to the ground.

"Relax. That's just an iron golem," Steve explained affectionately. "Local security force. They're a bunch of big softies unless you start messing with the villagers. Don't ever do that."

The iron golem leaned down to offer Natalie a red flower.

"This place makes no sense," Natalie said.

"I know," Henry said happily. "It's awesome."

The timer on Garrett's watch chimed. "Yo, I need some protein," he told Steve. "Like *now*."

Steve smiled. "I've got just the place, bro-hemoth." He led them to Steve's Hot Lava Chicken Shack in a bustling outdoor market. A bored villager stood behind the counter, waiting for customers.

"You ever wonder what happens when you mix hot lava and chicken?" Steve asked. "I did. And you're about to find out."

"Are we really taking a pit stop to feed the Garbage Man?" Natalie asked, eager to get back home.

"Sorry, sister," Garrett said, flexing his massive biceps. "You don't get these petting kittens. You get these taming lions!"

Steve pulled a lever. Hot lava cooked up a serving of chicken. "La-la-la-lava!" he sang as the chicken roasted in the lava. "Cha-cha-cha-chicken! Steve's lava chicken, crispy and juicy! Now we're having a snack! Ooh, super spicy, it's a lava attack!"

He took a big bite of chicken and immediately spat it out.

"AHHH! YAAAH! YAAAH! Way too hot! Hot hot hot hot HOT!!"

"Pass the bird," Garrett said, winking at Henry. "I'm not a wimp like Big Steve here. I crave heat, and I crave pain."

"Sir," Dawn observed, "you are a magnificent idiot."

Steve held up both hands. "Garrett, hear my words," he warned. "The chicken was just cooked with hot lava. Let it cool down, man!"

"No, give it to him," Natalie urged. "I'd love to see this."

Garrett took a piece of chicken. "See you on the other side," he said confidently. He bit into the chicken, chewed, nodded at Steve, swallowed, and grinned at Natalie.

"Not bad," Steve admitted, impressed.

They headed out. Garrett walked next to Henry. "Hey, Hank?" he said quietly, fighting tears. His face finally revealed the excruciating pain he was suffering. "Bro . . . bro. I think I burned my mouth really, really bad on that chicken. Can you find me, like, a snow cone or something?"

"Way ahead of you, dude," Henry replied, handing him a snow cone.

Garrett gobbled down the snow cone and took a

deep breath. "I never spit the chicken out, though. You saw that. I won. I won at chicken."

"Oh yeah," Henry agreed. "You're the best at chicken."

Garrett lowered his voice. "Hank, I'm gonna tell you something that I want to stay between us. Sometimes . . . I make bad decisions."

Henry laughed. Though he hadn't meant to be funny, Garrett smiled.

CHAPTER THIRTEEN

As the group moved on through Midport Village's square, Natalie asked Steve skeptically, "So how do we find this so-called Woodland Mansion?"

"Don't worry," Steve assured her. "I know the way. It's all up here." He pointed to his head. "Over the mountains, into the dark forest. Past loads of massive red mushrooms."

"Huge red mushrooms," Natalie said doubtfully. "Great. So you're just making this up. We need to find an actual map." She turned back and saw Henry and Garrett watching villager children jump on dozens of beds set up outside like trampolines. "Henry!" she called. "Let's go!"

"You know," Steve told her, "your brother has a gift. You should let him explore it. Creativity in this world is *key* to survival."

Natalie looked skeptical. "Well, that's not how it works in the real world. In the real world, creative kids get picked last in gym. They sit at the bummer lunch table. They get bullied. I can't let that happen to him. It's my job to protect him."

"Yup," Steve agreed, nodding. "That's exactly how I remember the real world, too."

"So maybe I belong in this one," Henry said. He'd caught up with them and overheard everything they'd said.

"Agreed," Steve said, smiling.

But Natalie definitely didn't agree. "Henry, don't even *say* that."

"Why?" Henry asked. "You're always telling me to grow up and then two seconds later telling me how much being grown-up stinks." Frustrated, he walked ahead.

Steve turned to Natalie. "Henry's not the one you're protecting, you know." He was implying that Natalie was really just protecting herself. Steve trotted ahead to join Henry. Natalie stood there, thinking. Could Steve be right? Was she just trying to protect herself, not Henry?

As he passed Natalie, Garrett said, "For the record, this is why I never had sisters."

Dawn caught up with Natalie. "Hey, you okay?" she asked. "Come on. I found some dude selling maps." They headed to the map stand together.

The three guys reached Steve's secret stash of supplies in the village's armory. Steve gestured toward stacks of equipment. "TNT, firework rockets, and blades for days," he said proudly. "Everything we'll need to make it to Woodland Mansion."

Looking around, Garrett said, "Don't love the layout. The karmic flow's all impacted, dude. Feel it in my wrists." He picked up a large blocky gem. "What's this junk?"

"That's an Ender pearl," Steve explained. "Teleports you to wherever you throw it."

"Yeah, right," Garrett snorted, not believing him. He tossed the pearl aside. In a cloud of purple particles, he instantly teleported to where the pearl landed.

"Aaaaand that was the only one I had," Steve said. "No biggie. Almost died fighting an Enderman for it." Garrett just stood there, dazed and confused by the experience of teleportation.

"What's an Enderman?" Henry asked curiously.

Steve made a face. "Nightmare fuel, kid. Hopefully you'll never meet one. Come with me!"

As Henry followed Steve, Garrett spotted a cracked antique cube among the pile of objects. It was roughly the size and shape of the Orb of Dominance. He looked at the antique cube, then looked at Henry's satchel, which held the Orb of Dominance.

And Garrett got an idea. . . .

At the map stand, Natalie and Dawn were having trouble communicating with the villager in charge of selling maps.

"Once again," Natalie repeated, "we need a *map* to the *Woodland Mansion*."

"Hrrrm," the map salesperson mumbled.

Dawn leaned toward Natalie. "I think now he just feels like you're talking down to him," she whispered.

Steve led Henry to a very cool-looking wooden block with a grid on its surface. "This is a crafting table," he said. "Here's how it works. You just place these elements on the table in different patterns"—he arranged a stick and two iron ingots on the slab—"and *KA-BOOM!*" Steve grabbed a hammer and slammed it into the center of the grid, transforming the elements into a beautiful sword. "You've got yourself a sweet blade!" he announced, setting down the hammer and lifting the sword to admire it.

He passed the sword to Henry, who turned it in the light, inspecting it. "This is incredible," he marveled. "Can I try?"

Steve extended his hand toward the table. "Sure!" he said. "Try making your own sword. You're gonna need it."

Searching the room, Henry chose several different pieces, then carefully arranged them on the crafting table. He smiled, enjoying creating something new.

WHAM! Henry hammered the grid, and the pieces were forged into a single object! He lifted it: a hybrid weapon combining a sword, an axe, and a mace, all covered in interesting design details. "Check it out—it's a battle-swax!" Henry said proudly, combining the words *sword* and *axe* into *swax*. He studied Steve's face, trying to read his reaction to the weapon. "I know I didn't do the assignment."

"No, you didn't," Steve agreed. Then he grinned broadly. "You did better: you *ignored the assignment.* You let your imagination run wild!"

Henry beamed. He'd been waiting a long time to hear someone say that.

CHAPTER FOURTEEN

Cracking his knuckles, Garrett stepped up to the crafting table. "You wanna see a blade?" he asked. "I'll show you a blade."

Without really having a clue of what he was doing, Garrett started wandering around the chamber, randomly gathering materials. "I was invited to join a ninja clan once," he bragged. "Because of my ability to move freely among the shadows. But you have to sacrifice everything and become nameless, and I just wasn't willing to do that."

"I know exactly what you mean, G-Man," Steve said, nodding. "Back in Idaho, I was a member of three ninja clans. My specialty was throwing stars. They called me Triple S for Star Man Steve. It's not easy fighting crime under the cloak of darkness. But sometimes you have to answer the call, and I was willing to do that."

Garrett haphazardly set some iron ingots on the

table. He took a mighty swing with the hammer, slamming it down on the grid. *CLANK.* The ingots were forged into . . . a bucket.

"That's okay, bud," Steve told him, patting his shoulder. "Buckets are useful here."

Garrett growled, scowling.

Henry stepped up to the table. "Hey, can I try something else?" No one said he couldn't, so he added some pieces to the bench and turned Garrett's bucket into *two* buckets attached by a thick-linked chain. He picked up his creation and handed it to Garrett. "Check it out."

Garrett swung the buckets around like nunchucks. "Not bad," he chuckled. "Not bad. Buck-chuckets."

Henry got another idea. "Can I try something else?" he asked Steve.

"Totally," Steve said. "Let it rip, Hank."

"Hey, that's what *I* call him!" Garrett objected.

Henry emptied his pockets. From the small pile of stuff, he picked out a nine-volt battery, a paper clip, the pink eraser Mr. Gunchie had tossed him in art class, and a tater tot.

"Pocket tots?" Garrett asked. "Dude, you had tots this whole time?"

Henry combined the four items from his pockets with elements from Steve's supplies, including a hunk of iron and a wooden stick, and arranged them all on the crafting table. *WHAM!* Steve and Garrett leaned in to see what Henry had crafted: a small cannon of some sort.

"Check it out," Henry said. "A Tot Launcher!" He fired a tot at the wall. *BOOM!* The tot exploded!

Steve was bowled over by Henry's creativity. "Dude, I never thought about doing that! You just used boring junk from the real world to craft something *amazing*! That's next-level!"

Pleased by Steve's praise, Henry inspected his Tot Launcher.

"Steve, come here a sec," Garrett said, pulling him aside. "There was a note with the Orb that said something about riches."

"Sure," Steve said, nodding. "There's riches everywhere. I keep a fat stash of diamonds at the Redstone Mines."

Greed shone in Garrett's eyes. "Nice. Is your treasure load on the way to this mansion place?"

Steve shook his head. "Not at all. It'd be a major detour. And the mines can be perilous."

Shrugging, Garrett said, "Guess we're gonna be making that detour, then." He opened his coat to show Steve he had the Orb of Dominance! While Henry was concentrating on crafting new items,

Garrett had swapped the cracked antique orb for the one in his satchel. "I'll make it simple for you," Garrett stated. "No diamonds, no Orb."

As Steve thought about Garrett's ultimatum, they both heard a low rumbling. The ground started to shake, and weapons fell to the floor. *CLANK!*

At the map stand, Natalie, Dawn, and all the villagers felt the shaking, too. They had no idea what was causing it, but it had to be something big.

"Is this normal?" Henry asked Steve nervously.

"No," Steve said. "This is bad." He hurried outside to see what was going on. Henry and Garrett followed him.

As they stepped out into the square, they saw a terrible horde of piglin soldiers, led by General Chungus, charging into the village!

Villagers scattered as Chungus raised his fist, setting his army loose. At the map stand, the vendor ran off. A piglin fired an arrow into a villager near Dawn and Natalie. *POOF!* The villager disintegrated!

Screaming, Natalie and Dawn pushed over a table and ducked behind it, using it as a shield. Arrows slammed into the table. *THWOCK! THWOCK! THWOCK! THWOCK!*

"Who . . . *what* are those things?" Garrett asked.

"Piglins," Steve answered. "They must be after

the Orb." As arrows whizzed by, Steve held up a shield. Garrett and Henry ducked behind him.

Chungus was barreling toward them, casually swatting villagers aside like pesky bugs. When he spotted Steve, he gave a friendly wave. "Hey, Steve! Good to see you, man! Just here to follow up about the Orb!"

"Crap." Steve sighed. "Chungus. Malgosha's double-crossed me!" Chungus was getting closer. Steve tossed his shield and brandished his sword. "Stand back, boys. This pig is mine!"

Garrett stepped in front of Steve, wanting to be the hero. "No! He's mine. I'm done with you getting all the glory around here." He spun his buck-chuckets wildly.

"Garrett, listen—" Steve started to say. *WHACK!* A bucket knocked Steve out cold.

CHAPTER FIFTEEN

"Steve!" Henry cried.

Chungus charged Garrett. Then . . . he stopped. Face to face with Garrett, Chungus told him, "Hey, man. We don't have to do this. I just need that orb."

"Sorry," Garrett said. "I don't negotiate with pigs." He swung his buckets, but Chungus easily knocked him down and dragged him off, screaming.

Thinking fast, Henry used his Tot Launcher against the other piglins. *THOMPF! THOMPF! THOMPF!* Aiming for the ground, he shot tots for the piglins to slip and slide on.

Chungus gave Garrett a mighty kick, sending him tumbling across the ground. Garrett sat up and tried to shake his head clear. Chungus was headed his way. "Tut, tut, tut, tut, tut . . . go on," Garrett said to himself.

Just as Chungus was about to deliver his knockout blow, an iron golem whacked him with both arms, sending him flying across Midport Village. The golem looked at Garrett, who nodded back to him. "Nice assist by me," Garrett said. He got up and ran back to Henry just as Steve was coming to.

"What happened?!" Steve asked, still a little groggy.

"I just saved your sorry butt," Garrett claimed. "You can thank me later."

The three of them ran off, chased by ferocious piglins.

Still in the middle of battling piglins herself, Natalie spotted Henry running off with Garrett and Steve. He turned and locked eyes with his sister for a moment, but there were way too many piglins between them. He had to keep running.

"Henry!" Natalie cried.

"We gotta go," Dawn told her. *"Now."*

"Dawn, I need him," Natalie pleaded. "He needs me."

"He needs you alive," Dawn said firmly. "Come on! We'll meet him at the Woodland Mansion."

"The map guy!" Natalie realized. "We gotta find him!"

"Let's roll!" Dawn said. They ran.

At the edge of the village, Steve, Henry, and Garrett ran up huge stone steps that led to the top of a cliff. Piglins were chasing them.

"Garrett, what about Natalie?" Henry panted.

"We'll meet her at the mansion!" Garrett promised.

Henry looked down at the piglins, who were gaining on them. He quickly knocked out some blocks and threw them down the steps, crafting a makeshift wall to slow their pursuers down.

They reached the edge of a cliff. Below lay a deep chasm. There was nowhere to go.

"What do we do now?" Henry asked, panicking.

"Only one move left," Steve said, pulling wingsuits out of his satchel. "Elytra wingsuits!" he exclaimed, slapping them onto Henry's and Garrett's backs. *VWOOOMP!* Large gray wings with a slightly purple sheen spread out behind them.

"Whoa!" Henry said, twisting around to examine the wings.

Back down the stone steps, the piglins broke through Henry's wall.

Steve pointed across the chasm. "Aim for those mountains!"

"Mountains?" Henry asked, confused. "But I thought we were headed to the Woodland Mansion!"

"Hank, don't question the adults," Garrett scolded.

"But—"

"Bye-bye," Garrett said, shoving him off the cliff.

"YAAAAAUUUGGH!" Henry screamed as he plummeted out of sight.

Garrett turned to Steve. "You *sure* these things work?"

"Absolutely," Steve promised.

"Good," Garrett said. "Otherwise, I think I just committed murder."

Soaring high into the air, Henry burst back into view. His terror had turned into awe. "Whoa!" he cried.

The piglins were about to reach Garrett and Steve. "Follow me!" Garrett ordered, jumping off the cliff.

Steve searched through his bag for another wingsuit but came up empty. "NO! I thought I grabbed three suits!"

He leapt off the cliff, landing on Garrett's back.

Henry glided through the air, getting the hang of the wingsuit and loving it. Garrett glided up next to him with Steve on his back steering him by yanking on his long hair.

Garrett was *not* loving it.

"No way, dude!" he groused. "Let go of my hair! I'm not some stallion for you to tame!"

"Just relax," Steve told him in a confident but

soothing voice. "Let my hips guide you. It's the only way!"

BOOM! A fireball exploded between them!

They looked back to see that they were being pursued by a fleet of ghasts, big flying creatures that looked like cubic hot-air balloons with dangling tentacles. Piglins rode in baskets suspended from the ghasts, driving them on by poking them with spears and shooting arrows at the Roundlings.

"Hank!" Steve shouted. "We'll have a better chance if we split up!"

"WHAT?!" Henry screamed.

CHAPTER SIXTEEN

Hating this plan, Henry soared off in a different direction from Garrett. A ghast followed him. Two big piglin brutes launched a small, zombified piglin at him. It clamped on to his leg.

"Ahhh!" Henry screamed, trying to shake the zombified piglin off his leg. "Get off me! GET OFF ME!"

He pulled out his trusty Tot Launcher and aimed it at the piglin. But just as he pulled the trigger, an arrow knocked the launcher, ruining his aim. The arrow came from a piglin with a crossbow. Henry used his Tot Launcher to blast the piglin out of the sky. *THOMPF! THOMPF! THOMPF!*

Before he could turn it back toward the piglin gripping his leg, the piglin knocked Henry's Tot Launcher out of his hands. He watched it tumble down . . . down . . . gone!

Steve and Garrett flew between two ghasts. "We

gotta go faster!" Steve yelled.

"You're too big of a payload!" Garrett argued.

Piglins in the baskets under both ghasts aimed their weapons. Steve leaned forward and Garrett quickly dove. *BOOM! BOOM!* The ghasts blasted each other and exploded!

On a high ridge, hog riders ran alongside Steve and Garrett. The riders had dark beards and mohawks. Two of them leapt off their hogs and landed on Garrett, knocking Steve around so he was hanging underneath. He held on for dear life. The riders punched Garrett and pulled his hair.

"OWW!" Garrett yelled. "What is happening?!"

Henry flew up next to his two friends. The zombified piglin was still grasping his leg, refusing to let go.

"Henry!" Steve shouted when he saw him.

Henry frantically pointed at the piglin. "I can't get it off me!"

"Use the rocket!" Steve advised.

"Oh yeah!" Henry said. He pulled a firework rocket out of his satchel and lit it.

FWOOOM!

The thrust of the rocket knocked the piglin off his leg and into the mouth of a ghast. Holding on to the rocket, Henry shot forward, zooming straight toward a narrow tunnel in the mountain ahead. "AAAHHHHH!" he screamed.

"He's got the right idea," Steve told Garrett. "Follow him through that tunnel!"

"Okay," Garrett said, swerving toward the small opening. "But it's going to be tight. Point your toes!"

As they entered the tunnel, the two hog riders were knocked off Garrett's back. *WHAP!*

On the other side of the tunnel, Henry lost control and crashed into them. With their wings tangled together, they fell toward the ground. Steve quickly pulled out a bucket and handed it to Henry. "Toss the water just before we land! It'll cushion our impact!"

Henry looked skeptical. Steve saw the doubt in Henry's eyes. "Trust me! Water bucket! RELEASE!"

Henry threw down the bucket. A splash pad blossomed below them! They fell onto it and rolled, unhurt. They still hadn't reached the Redstone Mountains, but they were much closer than before.

Back in Midport Village, General Chungus and his defeated army of piglins knelt before Malgosha, starting to zombify for lack of Nether wart. "General Chungus," the sorceress snarled, "you have failed me for the last time."

"Look, Your Highness," Chungus pleaded, "everyone here knows it wasn't my best day. But I've set myself some manageable fitness goals. Like eating more vegetables—"

"BRING OUT THE BEAST!" Malgosha called. A piglin messenger scurried up and whispered in her ear. "What do you mean you 'just have to put the brain in'?" The piglin whispered some more. "Yes, that's a big deal!" Malgosha roared. "GET IT DONE!"

The messenger hurried away.

"I have a question," Chungus said. "If I try to escape and fail, is it going to make my death worse? It's something I'd need to know now."

STOMP. STOMP. STOMP. STOMP.

The Great Hog was coming.

He was huge. Powerful. Ugly. Terrifying. With evil, glowing eyes.

"The Great Hog," Malgosha gushed affectionately. "My ultimate weapon. Finally complete." She nodded toward Chungus. "Rid me of this worthless loser."

The Great Hog charged up his weapon.

"Well, I have no regrets," Chungus said. "I left everything out on the field—"

ZAP! The Great Hog blasted the general into sizzling pork chops. Zombified piglins staggered toward the chops, hungry.

"Kill the Roundlings and bring me the Orb," Malgosha commanded the Great Hog. "Get rid of these zombified piglins. They're of no use to me."

As the Great Hog blasted fireballs at the zombified piglins, Malgosha laughed and took a sip of Nether wart.

On the river just outside Midport Village, the map seller floated along in a small boat, unaware that he was being followed. From the shore, Dawn spotted him. "There he is! I got eyes on him!" She and Natalie ran out onto an old dock.

"Get back here!" Natalie yelled at the map guy. "We need a map!"

The map seller ignored them.

"We need a boat," Dawn said. "This is when Henry would come in handy." She was thinking about how Henry seemed to be able to build just about anything in this strange world.

"Okay," Natalie said. "Well, I guess he'd do some of that weird tree magic. . . ." She leaned down and punched a few blocks out of the dock.

"Hurry!" Dawn urged. "Map Dude's floating away."

"This really hurts," Natalie said, rubbing her knuckles. "Does that mean it's working?" She stood up and tossed the blocks into the water, but they just floated away.

"Yeah, that's not a boat," Dawn observed. "That's just a bunch of blocks on the water." She picked up a rock and tossed it onto the grass. "Oh, look!" she said sarcastically. "I built a house!"

"I'm sorry!" Natalie said, about to explode with frustration. "I have no idea what I'm doing! I can't 'craft' or whatever!"

Dawn peered downriver. "Well, that monocled weirdo is getting away. We'd better run him down." She glanced back to Midport. "Let's get out of here before those pig monsters catch up with us." She took off running along the riverbank. Natalie followed her.

In the trees behind them, there was rustling and heavy breathing.

Someone, or some*thing,* was watching them. . . .

CHAPTER SEVENTEEN

Henry, Garrett, and Steve hiked toward the base of the Redstone Mountains.

"You've got some talking to do, buddy," Garrett told Steve. "Hank and I want some answers."

"Yeah," Henry agreed. "Like who's the evil sorceress you were talking about?"

"Are those pig monsters gonna continue to be an issue for us?" Garrett asked.

"I'm afraid so," Steve admitted. "The sorceress is a piglin queen called Malgosha. She rules over a dark world called the Nether. It's terrible. Nothing but hot lava and pig farts. The piglins are mindless brutes with no thoughts beyond gold."

"Gold?" Garrett asked, intrigued.

"Malgosha's waging a war on the Overworld," Steve continued. "She hates everything it stands for."

"How do you know that?" Henry asked.

"I was her prisoner for a long time," Steve said.

They walked on in silence for a few moments. Henry looked around at the amazing colorful landscape of the Overworld. "How could she hate this place?" he asked.

"Malgosha hates *true* creativity," Steve answered. "When she was just a little piglin, she tried showing her sculpture at the craft fair. But when she pulled off the sheet, revealing her sculpture, everyone laughed! You can guess what happened next. She became an evil queen. Her rage and humiliation became the source of her dark magic. If anyone tried to stand up to her, she blasted them into pork chops with her staff."

"Mmm," Garrett said, getting hungry again. "Pork chops."

"Malgosha couldn't create, so now she destroys," Steve said. "If she ever gets the Orb, she'll black out the sun. Nether wart will flourish. This beautiful world, and everything in it, will wither and die. It'll all be Nether. Forever."

"And you were going to bring the Orb to her?" Henry asked accusingly. "Great idea."

"Of course I'm not going to give it to her!" Steve said defensively. "But I need the Orb for leverage." He sounded desperate. "I need to save Dennis."

Henry looked resolved. He'd grown to love the

Overworld and didn't want it destroyed. "We *can't* give the Orb to Malgosha," he said firmly. He turned to Garrett. "Maybe that's the real reason we're here. The Orb didn't bring us to find treasure. Maybe we're here to save this place."

Garrett looked unconvinced. He still needed money to save his business. "I bet we can do both," he said.

Steve looked up at the mountain looming before them. "The Woodland Mansion is just beyond the Redstone Mountains," he explained. "We can go over or through." He pointed at the entrance to a mine.

"Whichever is fastest," Henry said. "We gotta get to that mansion. Natalie will find us there. I know it."

Garrett shot Steve a look that said *Remember our deal—we go through the mines so I can load up on diamonds. Or else no Orb!*

Steve got the message. "Through will be faster."

"Okay," Henry said, "it's a plan." He pulled something gold out of his bag. "Hey, Garrett," he said shyly. "I made this for you at the village. Just to say thanks. You were the only person in Chuglass who was even a little cool to me."

"Thanks," Garrett said, taking the gold object but feeling awkward about it. Henry walked on.

Garrett examined his gift. It was a trophy with his face on it, the likeness taken from one of his flyers. And it was inscribed BEST BUD OF THE YEAR. He smiled.

As he put the trophy in his coat pocket, he felt the orb he'd swiped from Henry's satchel. He looked at the boy walking in front of him and experienced an unfamiliar sensation.

Could it be . . . guilt?

CHAPTER EIGHTEEN

Natalie and Dawn made their way along the riverbank. With nightfall, zombies and skeletons had emerged.

"Okay," Natalie said. "So we lost the map guy. I can't find my brother. And we have no clue where the Woodland Mansion is. We're really killing it." She smacked a skeleton in the face with a shovel. *WHACK!*

"This isn't your fault, Nat," Dawn assured her. "I work with pigs. If they wanna have a war, there's not much we can do about it." She smashed a zombie. *WHAM!*

Natalie sighed. "My only job is to keep Henry safe, and I'm blowing it. I promised my mom I'd never let anything happen to him. But I'm clearly not cut out for this parenting stuff." *WHACK!* Another zombie went down. "I just would have liked to have been a kid for a little bit longer, you know? Just to have that feeling like I could have done anything."

"I hear you," Dawn agreed. "Being a grown-up stinks. You get all these responsibilities. And you stop chasing your dreams." She whaled on another zombie. *BAM! THWACK! CLONK!* "You think I like having fifteen hustles? I'd kill to be like your brother. He's weird, but he just kinda goes for it. . . ."

"Maybe we're doing it wrong," Natalie suggested. "Aren't you supposed to, like, do what you love?"

Hitting a skeleton with a shovel, Dawn said, "I love my animals. I want to do that forever. But what if it doesn't work out? What if I go all in and it blows up in my face? That's what I like about your brother. He just tries stuff. I don't know. I feel like I just need a sign."

They heard rustling in the woods nearby. A large creature emerged. . . .

A wolf.

It slowly crept toward Dawn and Natalie, growling. They backed away.

Lifting her shovel, Natalie tried to sound tough. "You want some, too, big boy?!"

"Hey, hey, hey," Dawn said, putting up both hands. "Let's just calm down." She approached the wolf slowly, picking up a skeleton bone along the way. "This guy just needs a little TLC. Don't ya, big fella?" She offered the bone to the wolf, who sniffed it, then happily took it and munched on it. He sat up straight, cocked his head, and panted happily, his long tongue flapping out of his mouth.

"Look at you," Dawn said sweetly, cautiously ruffling his fur. "You are one beautiful doggo."

Natalie was impressed. "I cannot believe you just did that."

As Dawn petted the wolf, a blocky collar appeared around his neck. *POOF!* She read the name on the collar. " 'Dennis'? Steve's Dennis?"

Dennis barked twice. "WOOF! WOOF!"

"Can you . . . take us to him?" Dawn asked.

Dennis bolted a few steps ahead, then stopped and looked back as if to ask the women if they were coming.

Natalie and Dawn followed Dennis.

CHAPTER NINETEEN

Steve led the way through the Redstone Mines, following railway tracks and passing old machinery. "See all that glowy stuff?" he asked. "It's redstone. Conducts energy. You can build some pretty crazy contraptions with it." He tapped a stone and it glowed brighter. Henry mined some redstone ore, which left behind redstone dust. He smiled at the ore and dust, enchanted.

"Thought this was a *diamond* mine," Garrett grumbled. Red rocks that glowed and conducted energy weren't going to save his store.

"Easy, big dog," Steve reassured him. "They're here. If all you crave is material wealth, you shall have it."

"That has not been true so far in my life, but okay," Garrett said, keeping his eyes peeled for diamonds as they hiked deeper into the mine.

"I set a series of booby traps long ago, so we

must be careful," Steve warned. "Slime-and-piston powered." He looked around. "The first trap is, I wanna say . . ."

Garrett stepped on a pressure plate, releasing cactus balls! The prickly balls fired into his back, arms, and butt. "YEEAAAUUUGH!" he screamed.

"Right!" Steve cried, remembering. "I designed this one to hit the person who hangs out in the back of the pack—basically to punish cowardice."

"Get them off me!" Garrett yelled, flailing at the cactus balls and backing into a slime piston.

BLOOOOSH!

The piston blasted Garrett up into a series of slime traps high on the rocky walls. He pinballed around painfully until he finally fell onto a lever that opened a secret door to Steve's secret diamond stash!

"Ah! Here it is," Steve said. "Thanks, Garrett!"

Moaning, Garrett gave a weak thumbs-up.

Inside the hidden chamber, they saw gleaming piles of precious gems and diamonds. "What are we doing here?" Henry asked. "I thought the idea was to reach the Woodland Mansion as quickly as possible."

"Just a little pit stop, Hank," Garrett told him, pulling out a bag and gleefully stuffing jewels into it. "This is what I'm talking about!"

"Wait," Henry said, realizing, "did you two *plan* this?"

"I kinda let Steve know who was in charge," Garrett said, jamming as many gems as possible into his sack. "Believe me, he understood."

Glaring furiously at Garrett, Steve apologized. "I'm sorry, Henry."

"This was *always* the plan, Hank," Garrett claimed. "Remember why we came through the portal in the first place?"

Henry couldn't believe what he was hearing. "But we could be at the mansion already! Natalie and Dawn could *be* there! They could be in danger!"

Steve sniffed the air. "Oh no. Do you smell that? Nether wart!"

"What does that mean?" Henry asked.

Dust fell from the ceiling. They heard grunts. Someone was trying to break into the chamber. . . .

"No," Steve gasped, horrified. "The Great Hog! She finally put the brain in! RUN!"

Henry pointed to an empty minecart. The three of them ran toward it and jumped in. Garrett pushed the lever and the cart zipped away.

The cart rolled into a pitch-black cavern and slowed to a crawl. "Dang! The wind blew my torch out!" Steve cried.

"Whoa, why are we stopping?" Henry asked, concerned.

"We're a husky load, gents," Steve informed them. "We need a redstone boost. Fast."

"What's that sound?" Garrett asked. He lit a torch and saw that they were surrounded by creepers, the little four-legged guys who exploded at the slightest touch.

"My creeper farm," Steve explained.

"What kind of idiot would *breed* these things?!" Garrett demanded.

Henry pointed ahead. "Look! A powered rail!" When they reached the redstone arrow, they'd get another burst of power. But the cart was barely moving. And they could hear the Great Hog and his piglins approaching fast!

"Garrett," Henry said quickly, "you got us into this mess! Get out and push!"

"I can do that," Garrett said, climbing out of the cart. "I never skip leg day. Thick thighs save lives." He got behind the cart and pushed them forward.

"If one creeper goes off, will they all?" Henry asked.

"Oh yeah," Steve affirmed. "Big-time chain reaction. Push, Gar-Gar! Henry, start slapping those creepers!"

Henry reached down and started slapping creepers as the cart passed them. Steve did the same, activating the creepers. They started to vibrate and flash.

The Great Hog crashed into the cavern.

"Sure hope this timing works," Henry said.

"Me too, young friend," Steve agreed. It was crucial that they escape the chamber before all the creepers went off! Garrett needed to push them toward the powered rail to boost their speed.

Garrett pushed hard. They were just about to reach the powered rail.

"Get in! Get in!" Henry urged.

Garrett jumped into the cart just as it hit the arrow and zoomed out of the creeper farm, leaving the piglins surrounded by activated creepers. The piglins looked worried.

In no time, the cart shot out of the mountain into the bright sunshine. Then . . .

BOOOOOOM!

The whole mountain exploded, propelling the cart forward another fifty yards. The force of the blast fluttered the skin on the guys' faces.

CHAPTER TWENTY

The minecart slowly rolled to a stop. Feeling a little dizzy, the three guys climbed out.

"Nice work, Gar-Gar," Steve said sarcastically. "Your little detour almost got us killed!"

"Don't be so dramatic." Garrett shrugged. "We're alive."

Henry shoved Garrett, furious. "We didn't need those diamonds!" he fumed. "You almost got us killed! You're the most selfish person I've ever met."

"Whatever. I need them," Garrett said quietly. Then he spoke louder, his voice rising in frustration. "I need the diamonds to get the money. I'm broke, kid! You have no idea what it's like!"

"What are you talking about?" Henry asked.

Garrett decided to come clean. "My life sucks. I'm a loser, okay? There. I said it." He took a deep breath and let it out. "I know it seems like I've got it all figured out. Smart. Funny. Bilingual. Humble to a fault. But the reality? It's bad. I'm washed up, Hank. I'm gonna lose everything. And that's not the worst part. I'm alone."

"You *weren't* alone," Henry said, hurt. "I was your friend." He walked away.

Garrett just stood there, dumbstruck.

"Sorry to hear about your finances," Steve said after a moment of silence.

"Shut up, Steve," Garrett growled.

Dennis led the way out of the forest and into a field. This part of the Overworld struck Natalie as having the prettiest view she'd seen so far. In the distance, she spotted a big red mushroom. "Huge red mushrooms," she marveled. "So Steve's *not* crazy. Well, not about this, anyway. You know, this place is starting to grow on me."

"Yeah, this is real nice. You could turn one of those big mushrooms into a time-share tree house," Dawn said, following Dennis toward a path flanked by red mushrooms, which led to the Woodland Mansion.

Meanwhile, Steve, Henry, and Garrett had made their way from the exploded Redstone Mountain to the Woodland Mansion. Just outside the mansion, they assessed the situation. "There it is," Steve said. "The Woodland Mansion. We're gonna get in, get the Earth Crystal, and get you guys home!" He went on to brief Henry and Garrett on what lay inside the massive structure. He'd built a very rough model of the mansion with wood blocks and scraps. "Pay close attention to Papa Steve," he instructed. "There are three floors. The first floor is full of vindicators."

From the looks on their faces, it was clear that Henry and Garrett had no idea what vindicators were.

"Axe murderers, basically," Steve explained, moving little figurines made of sticks.

"Are these supposed to be different things?" Garrett asked, picking up one of the figures. "They all look the same."

Steve snatched the figure back. "Button it up, Garrett! The second floor crawls with evokers. They wield powerful dark magic." He picked up a different figurine and made it float through the air.

"Yeah, yeah," Garrett said impatiently. "Wizards on the top floor. That's just basic video game math."

"Oh yeah, Garrett knows everything," Henry said, rolling his eyes.

"How long are you going to be mad at me, dude?!"

"I *just* got mad at you!" Henry snapped.

"Well, I don't love it," Garrett told him.

"You should have thought of that before you almost got us killed," Henry said.

"I'm sorry, Hank," Garrett said, meaning it. "Truly."

Henry glared at him. "My name's not Hank."

"One more thing," Garrett continued, wanting to get it all out. "And I hate myself for this. Promise you won't get more mad."

"I don't see how I could," Henry said.

"It's a bad one," Garrett said. "I stole the Orb while you were crafting." He pulled it out of his pocket and offered it to Henry. "Here. We cool . . . Henry?"

Henry just stared at the Orb in disbelief. "You are literally the worst human being on the face of—"

"Henry, we'll give this guy the business later, okay?" Steve interrupted, wanting to get to the matter at hand. He drew their attention back to his makeshift model. "Now, both of you, eyes on my demonstraysh. The third floor houses the loot chamber. That's where the Earth Crystal is."

"The boxy thing the Orb goes into?" Garrett asked.

"Exactly," Steve confirmed. " 'The boxy thing the

Orb goes into.' It's guarded by Endermen. Whatever you do, *do not look them in the eye.*"

"I can build stairs to the second floor," Henry said. "I'll sneak in through a window, get up to the third floor, and snag the Earth Crystal."

Garrett nodded slowly, genuinely impressed. "Good idea, Hank."

"But to pull it off, we'd need a pretty sweet diversion," Steve pointed out.

"You know what would work really well on these guys?" Garrett suggested. "It's gonna sound crazy, but a big-time friendship jamboree."

Steve's eyes lit up. "Did you just say 'a big-time friendship jamboree'?"

"You heard me," Garrett responded.

"You have no idea how long I've been waiting for someone to say that," Steve said, smiling, his eyes aglow. Garrett smiled, too, happily surprised by Steve's reaction.

It was time for a big-time friendship jamboree!

CHAPTER TWENTY-ONE

CREEEEAK...

The front door to the mansion opened slowly. Disguised as singing telegram delivery guys in little hats and uniforms, Steve and Garrett danced, stepping back and forth and side to side.

"Hey, hey, hey!" Garrett said in a super-cheerful voice. "Did someone order a saxophone birthday party?"

Holding up a saxophone, Steve chimed in. "Oh yeah! We heard there's a birthday boy in the house! Which one of you lucky guys is Reggie? If one of you is Reggie, just stand there glaring at us menacingly."

On the other side of the door, a crowd of vindicators stared from under heavy, dark brows, brandishing their iron axes. Their skin was gray, and their faces were fierce.

Garrett and Steve launched into a lively birthday rap, providing just the diversion Henry needed to craft a stairway, climb up to the second floor, and slip through a window unnoticed. At the end of a hallway, he spotted stairs leading up to the third floor.

But evokers—the dark wizards Steve had warned them about—roamed the hallway, entering and exiting rooms. With gray skin and heavy brows, they looked similar to the vindicators but wore long black robes trimmed in gold. "Gotta time it right," Henry muttered to himself.

The evokers all stepped into rooms, leaving the hallway clear. Henry ran, reaching the stairway before the evokers returned.

Back at the front door, Garrett and Steve were running out of improvised lyrics to their birthday rap. "Friendship is the wish you make when you blow out the candles on your birthday cake—" Garrett turned to Steve and said in a quick aside, "I almost want them to kill us so we don't have to do this anymore."

"We gotta switch it up fast!" Steve agreed. "They don't look happy."

The vindicators were starting to lift their axes.

Steve launched into a new tune on his saxophone called "Crazy Train." Then he pulled the sax out of his mouth and announced, "All aboard! Let's get those tickets out! Because we're going on a TRAIN RIDE!"

He started singing "Crazy Train" with all the energy he could muster, hoping to hold the vindicators' attention long enough for Henry to complete his mission. Garrett joined in, singing and dancing as Steve clapped his hands and wailed on the saxophone. Performing together, they weren't bad!

But the vindicators had heard enough. They were *not* big music fans. They moved toward Steve and Garrett. . . .

Up on the third floor, Henry crept toward the loot chamber. He heard a floorboard creak behind him. He looked back to see an evoker gesturing with its hands, casting a spell. A swarm of vexes—evil beings with iron swords—flew through the air toward Henry!

"Of course they have swords," he said to himself as he turned to run.

He bolted for the door to the loot chamber with the vexes shrieking after him. Just in time, he dove through and slammed the door behind him.

SLAM!

When he turned around and saw what was in the loot chamber, Henry said, "You're kidding me."

Chests. Lots and lots of chests. Stacked high and

deep. An overwhelming number of chests to search through.

Downstairs, the vindicators had forced Garrett and Steve into a fighting arena. Steve was tied to a corner of the ring, but Garrett was free to face his opponent . . .

. . . a chicken.

The vindicators surrounded the arena, cheering and yelling.

"Steve?" Garrett asked, utterly baffled. "What's going on? Do they want me to fight this chicken?"

"Yeah, I think this is some sort of vindicator fight club," Steve answered. "I've heard about these, but I've never seen one." He looked around the large chamber. "This is a pretty impressive build. Nice lighting, solid boxing ring."

Garrett shrugged and raised his fists. "I guess it's him or me, then. . . ."

A box lowered from the ceiling. The bottom swung open, and a baby zombie fell out, landing on the chicken like a soldier mounted on a horse.

"What the . . . ," Garrett said, even more baffled. "It's like a . . ."

". . . chicken jockey," Steve said.

SSSSSSSS! Hissing, the baby zombie charged at Garrett, knocking him into a corner of the ring. It chomped its large teeth, trying to bite him. *CLACK! CLACK! CLACK!*

"Hey, hey, hey!" Garrett protested. "No biting!"

"It's a fight to the death!" Steve shouted. "There are no rules!"

As Garrett struggled to hold the chomping baby zombie at arm's length, the chicken bit his leg. "STOP ANNOUNCING AND HELP ME!" Garrett yelled at Steve. Swinging through the ropes, the baby pummeled Garrett ferociously.

In the loot chamber, Henry opened chest after chest, searching for the Earth Crystal. "Come on, come on," he muttered anxiously. Opening yet another chest, he found a diamond axe glowing purple. He decided to take it, figuring it might come in handy. Then he spotted a box on the other side of the room emitting a blue light from its interior. As he hurried toward it, tall, thin figures with glowing eyes slipped across the room behind Henry.

Endermen.

Downstairs, the baby zombie was smashing Garrett's head. He broke free and said to Steve, "Please don't ever tell anyone about this!" Then he kicked the baby in the face. *THUNK!*

The baby flew through the air, landed on its butt, and started to cry pathetically.

"Look, I'm sorry," Garrett said, feeling bad. "Don't cry. . . ." He approached the little zombie to comfort it, but it stopped crying, clamped on to Garrett's hand with its teeth, and flipped him onto his back. *WHAM!* The vindicators cheered wildly!

"Keep doing what you're doing!" Steve urged Garrett. "You got this, big man!" As he cheered Garrett on, Steve concentrated on wriggling out of the ropes that bound him.

Upstairs, Henry opened the chest with the blue light and found . . . the Earth Crystal! He picked it up, stared at the awesome object, and stowed it in his satchel.

Looking up, he noticed a dark shape reflected in a window. When he whipped around, the shadowy figure was gone, leaving only purple particles drifting in the air.

POOF! The teleporting Enderman reappeared right in front of Henry!

It was tall and black, with a cubic head, two long arms, two long legs, and two glowing purple eyes that Henry couldn't help but stare into. Slowly, the Enderman opened its rectangular mouth . . .

. . . and screamed!

Henry grabbed his temples. His eyes glowed purple. Disturbing images filled his brain.

Garrett looked through Henry's sketchbook, laughing at his drawings. "This stuff is trash, kid!" he mocked.

"You don't belong here, Henry," Steve said, his face looking twisted and mean. "You don't belong anywhere!"

"This is all your fault," Natalie said, looking just as cruel as Steve had. "Now we'll never see each other again!"

In his childhood home, Henry's mother spoke to him accusingly. "Natalie is in danger. You put all your friends and this entire world in danger. Why?" She held up Henry's idea sketchbook. "Because you thought you were special? That the world cared what was in your little mind?" She tossed the sketchbook into the fireplace, where logs were blazing.

"Grow up, Henry," she said.

CHAPTER TWENTY-TWO

Henry snapped out of the Enderman's nightmare. His eyes stopped glowing purple. He shook his head, trying to get his bearings. His visions had seemed so *real*.

He saw the Enderman still standing right in front of him, its eyes glowing purple. Ducking low, Henry swung his enchanted diamond axe at the Enderman's legs, knees, torso, and, finally, as it bent over, its square head. *POOF!* An Ender pearl fell. Henry scooped it up, then smashed his axe into the floor. *CRASH!* He dropped through to the story below.

Meanwhile, in the fighting arena, the baby zombie had climbed onto the post at the corner of the boxing ring. It was preparing to leap on Garrett and finish him off. The crowd of vindicators was going wild.

"No . . . ," Garrett pleaded, holding up his hand. "No . . ."

As the baby launched itself off the post, Garrett braced himself. But out of nowhere, Steve appeared, kicking the zombie in midair and sending it flying! The vindicators were stunned. Steve helped Garrett to his feet.

"You saved me," Garrett said in disbelief.

"That's what friends do, Garrett," Steve said. They grabbed the backs of each other's necks and pressed their foreheads together.

"Any time, any place, anywhere," Garrett vowed. "I'll always be there for you."

The chicken jumped up and tried to attack Steve, but he just grabbed it by the neck and tossed it out the window. The baby zombie returned, hungry for vengeance.

"Let's do this," Steve told Garrett. Together, they put an awesome tag-team wrestling move on the baby zombie, taking him out of action. Celebrating their win, they did an elaborate handshake that looked like a dance, bumping fists, touching elbows, waggling fingers, and swinging their hips.

Garrett jumped onto the ropes and bellowed, "This is NOT pro wrestling! You people are SICK!"

"Where's Henry?" Steve asked.

SMASH! Using his diamond axe, Henry broke through the ceiling and dropped into the ring. He stood up and looked around, a little confused.

"Hank!" Garrett cried happily.

"Did you get the Earth Crystal?" Steve asked eagerly.

Henry held up his satchel. "Yup. Got it."

"Attaboy, Henry!" Steve said, clapping him on the back. "Now let's find Natalie and Dawn!"

The three of them ran out, leaving the stunned crowd of vindicators to ponder what had just happened. Henry, Steve, and Garrett burst out the front door of the Woodland Mansion and ran across a huge bridge spanning the deep canyon surrounding the building.

But as they crossed the bridge, something rose out of the mist. . . .

Ghasts! They were carrying gondolas piloted by piglins, just like the ones Steve, Garrett, and Henry had escaped from in the chasm outside Midport Village. The ghasts rose on both sides of the bridge, surrounding them!

Below, on the most elaborate ghast gondola, rode the Great Hog—who had somehow survived the creeper explosion in the mines—and Malgosha.

"Oh no," Steve moaned. "It's her."

The piglin sorceress raised her staff and sucked the Orb right out of Henry's satchel. To the guys' horror, the Orb flew straight to the top of her staff. Malgosha cackled with evil triumph.

"No!" Henry cried.

"Kill them!" Malgosha commanded. "We have work to do." She flew off, leaving her minions to do her nasty bidding.

Dozens of multicolored piglins carrying mushroom bombs leapt onto the bridge.

"Seeker piglins!" Steve gasped. "They're gonna blow this bridge sky-high!"

Lowering his voice, Garrett nodded toward a ghast and asked Steve, "Could you get on one of those demon marshmallow things?"

Steve looked. The ghast's gondola was about twelve feet below the bridge. The basket was small, but it looked as though it could hold two human passengers. He nodded.

Garrett grabbed Henry by his shirt and the seat of his pants and tossed him into the empty gondola dangling below the ghast. Steve took off running and leapt into the gondola next to Henry. "Slime block!" he called as he threw one down for Garrett to jump onto.

Henry and Steve looked up at Garrett, surrounded by seeker piglins closing in on him with their mushroom bombs.

"Go, Hank," Garrett called down to them. "Save Dawn and your sister and get home."

"Garrett, come on!" Steve urged. "Jump!"

"No! Get outta here!" Garrett said. "Tell my story in song. Heavy metal, please. Real instruments."

"You don't have to do this!" Henry pleaded. "I forgive you! Remember what you said! Dead dudes can't win Gamer of the Year!"

Garrett smiled the most genuine smile Henry'd ever seen him make. "I already have a trophy, kid."

The seeker piglins swarmed over Garrett. As he fought them, the ghast flew off.

"NO!!!" Henry screamed.

BOOOOM!

The seeker piglins' mushroom bombs exploded! The bridge was gone. Pork chops rained down into the chasm.

Flying away under the ghast, Henry and Steve mourned their lost friend, aching with sadness. But after a few moments, Steve spoke. "Henry, I know we're both hurting, but there's something important I need to tell you. I don't know how to land these things."

WHAM!

They crashed into a tree, and everything went black.

Henry opened his eyes and saw . . . Natalie! She smiled, then hugged him tight.

Dawn was there, too. She'd reunited Steve and Dennis. The two best friends were slobbering all over each other.

"Dennis!" Steve cried joyfully. "Man, did I miss you!"

"Dennis is a dog?" Henry asked.

Dennis growled. "Grrrr . . ."

"Wolf, dude," Steve corrected him. He turned back to his best buddy. "I was so scared I lost you, boy. What happened? Where were you?"

Dennis went into a long explanation of barks, howls, growls, and whimpers.

Smiling warmly, Steve said, "You saved the whole Overworld, Dennis. You were so brave. But now we gotta do it again. You up for it?"

"ARRRROOOO!" Dennis howled in agreement.

"Now I understand why you kept yourself so filthy and smelly," Dawn said. "So Dennis would find you one day."

"Exactly," Steve confirmed proudly.

"I was so afraid you were dead," Henry told his big sister.

"I'm right here," she assured him. "I'm not going anywhere."

Henry sighed. "I'm sorry, Nat. Everything's my fault. Garrett's gone. And we're stuck here."

"I'm so sorry," Natalie said, pulling him in for another big hug.

"Garrett died a true hero," Steve said solemnly. "Honestly, I'm a little jealous."

CHAPTER TWENTY-THREE

"Henry, look at me," Natalie said gently. Her brother raised his eyes to hers, looking miserable. "Don't blame yourself. And don't start doubting yourself, not now. You were *right* about this place."

Nodding, Henry felt a little better. He looked around. They seemed to be inside some kind of structure. "Hold on. Where are we?"

"I kinda made a little safe house thing," Natalie explained humbly.

Wanting to get a better look at the building, Henry ran outside. Natalie watched him from the open doorway. He saw that she had crafted a colorful tower shaped like a mushroom, showing off her creativity and imagination. "Nat," Henry said, impressed, "you did it!"

"Yeah," Natalie said, beaming. "It's not as good as yours, of course. But I'm proud of it."

Henry beamed back at her. He could tell from

her smile that Natalie was finally experiencing the good feeling he'd often felt when he'd created something new.

But suddenly, he experienced a flashback of his nightmarish encounter with the Enderman. His eyes went purple. He clutched his temples in pain.

"Henry?" Natalie asked, hurrying to his side. She helped him back into her mushroom tower. Once inside, Henry tried to explain what he was going through. "At the mansion, this creature gave me a horrible vision. It was Mom telling me to *give up*."

Steve told him, "That wasn't your mom, Henry. The Endermen are liars. And they know how to use our greatest fears against us."

"You know what Mom wanted for you," Natalie said. "*Use* your gifts. Maybe make the world a little better."

Henry smiled.

FWOOOOOM!

A deafening sound pulled them all to the window to see what was going on outside. They saw a beam of purple light shooting straight up into the blocky sun!

"It's begun," Steve said grimly. "The Great Darkening. Malgosha's gathering all her forces. The Overworld won't stand a chance."

"Unless we fight for it," Henry said.

Natalie nodded.

"Gonna be a lot of killer pigs down there," Dawn mused. "I think I can get us some reinforcements."

"Yes!" Steve exclaimed. Then he looked doubtful. "From where?"

"Leave that to me," Dawn told him.

"I have an idea for kind of a crazy build," Henry said. "Nat?"

"I can help with that," she said. Henry smiled. He liked the idea of crafting something with his sister. He turned to Steve. "I'll need some serious resources."

Steve tossed him a pickaxe. "All right, listen up! I'm gonna need someone to *mine,* and I'm gonna need someone to *craft.* LET'S MINECRAFT!"

Over the meadow near the portal back to Earth, the sky darkened. Sheep looked up, wondering what was going on.

The same gloom was spreading across the sky over Midport Village. Villagers stopped what they were doing and stared.

At the edge of the forest, the mobs of skeletons

and zombies that normally came out only at night began to emerge in the unnatural darkness.

And at the massive portal between the Nether and the Overworld, netherrack blocks spread out, turning the grass and stone dull red. From the blocks, Nether wart fungus sprouted. Heavily armed piglin troops marched out of the portal, urged on by their sorceress queen.

"Today we take the Overworld as ours!" Malgosha declared. "Attack the village! Burn their homes and symmetrical farms. All they've created . . . we destroy!"

All the piglins cheered with menacing oinks, grunts, and squeals.

Malgosha turned to a brigade of piglins carrying lit torches and pointed her staff at Midport Village in the distance. "CHARGE!"

CHAPTER TWENTY-FOUR

On a nearby rise, Henry crafted stacks of iron blocks. Natalie slapped pumpkin heads on them. They came to life as iron golems!

Henry pulled purple Boots of Swiftness onto the final golem, turning it into a super golem with the power of great speed.

"Fools!" Malgosha laughed when she saw what the siblings were doing. "Iron golems will not attack unless provoked!"

PLINK.

An arrow shot by one of the piglins hit an iron golem and harmlessly bounced off. The iron golems all turned their heads toward the rider.

Malgosha sighed. "You gotta be kidding me."

The iron golems charged down the hill and into the hoglin calvary, swinging their long arms to knock the riders off their hogs. The super golem loomed over the piglin that had shot the arrow and whacked him into the sky. Dozens of skeletons, zombies, and spider jockeys rushed into the fight, swarming the iron golems, who smashed and swatted them.

"You sure those boots work?" Natalie asked Henry as he activated them.

WHOOSH!

The super golem blasted off at an incredible speed.

"Yeah, I think they work," Henry answered, following the super golem as it cleared a path to the portal. The brother and sister fought the piglins side by side, Natalie with her sword and Henry with his new Tot Launcher.

Meanwhile, Steve crept up behind Malgosha, placed blocks on the ground, jumped on the blocks, and launched himself into the air.

"SNEAK ATTACK!"

Malgosha whipped around to face Steve and saw that he was wearing diamond armor and carrying a diamond sword. "Huh?!"

With his diamond sword drawn, Steve flew through the air, but he belly-flopped onto the ground short of Malgosha, who immediately attacked him with her staff. Leaping to his feet, Steve flung eggs at her.

"EGG ATTACK!"

When the eggs hit the sorceress, they turned into baby chicks. Steve built a small block wall and jumped at it, crying, "PARKOUR ATTACK!" Using his best parkour moves, he twisted and spun off the wall, crashing into Malgosha. They clashed, battling each other with every tactic they could think of.

As the fighting raged on, Henry and Natalie approached the tall portal to the Nether, which rose several stories above them. Atop the portal sat the Orb of Dominance, projecting its purple beacon of darkness into the sky. A new wave of piglins was fast approaching.

Smiling, Henry pulled out the Ender pearl he'd obtained on the third floor of the Woodland Mansion by defeating the Enderman. He loaded it into a launcher.

"Do it, Henry," Natalie said. "I got this. . . ." Raising her sword, she turned to face the horde of running piglins.

Henry carefully aimed for the top of the portal.

FOOMPH!

The Ender pearl shot out of the barrel and flew through the air to the top of the portal.

FWOOSH!

Teleported by the Ender pearl, Henry appeared atop the portal next to the Orb of Dominance in its beacon of darkness. Natalie braced herself for the oncoming piglins. But then she heard a familiar voice. . . .

"HEY, YOU STUPID PIGS!" Dawn shouted. "OVER HERE!"

Dawn and Dennis emerged from a stand of trees. She turned to the eager wolf. "Sic 'em, Dennis!" He tore off.

Dawn whistled, and dozens of wolves sprinted out of the trees to join Dennis. These were the reinforcements Dawn had mentioned. She'd successfully recruited them using her strong connection to all animals. The flood of wolves charged into the piglins to protect Natalie.

Seeing the super golem clearing a way to the portal, the Great Hog charged into battle, firing his blaster at the iron golems.

ZZWORK!

His crackling bolts of energy proved much more effective against the iron golems than the hog riders' arrows. But the super golem zipped over to the Great Hog and knocked him around like a soccer ball.

WHAM!

WHACK!

Spotting Henry up on the portal, the Great Hog managed to blast a fireball his way. *ZWOOOMP!*

Just as he was about to grab the Orb, Henry was knocked off!

"Henry!" Natalie screamed. She and Dawn watched in helpless horror. Steve, still fighting Malgosha, looked up and saw Henry fall.

Screaming, Henry plummeted ten stories through the air! "AAAAUUUGH!"

CHAPTER TWENTY-FIVE

Out of nowhere, Garrett swooped down, piloting a ghast from the gondola hanging underneath it! He caught Henry before he hit the ground and hauled him in.

"I got you, partner!" Garrett crowed.

"Garrett!" Henry exclaimed, overjoyed. "You're alive!"

Garrett winked. "Molten Hot Garbage Tip Number One: Winners never die. Plus, I remembered that sweet water bucket trick you used. Breaks your fall every time!" Steering the ghast into a U-turn over Natalie and Dawn, Garrett flew back toward the portal.

Dawn and Natalie were thrilled to see that Garrett had somehow survived his fall off the Woodland Mansion bridge. But more skeletons and zombies were emerging from the woods! Something had to be done to stop the oncoming darkness!

In the gondola, Garrett shouted, "LET IT RIP, HANK!" Henry poked the ghast with a spear. The ghast launched a flurry of fireballs at the portal. *BOOM!* The portal tower crumbled, and the Orb of Dominance tumbled to the ground, ending the Great Darkening. Night turned to day, and the creatures of the night burst into flame!

"No!!!" Malgosha cried.

The Great Hog picked up the Orb of Dominance, laughing at Natalie and Dawn. But before he could return it to Malgosha, the Great Hog was slammed by the super golem zooming in with its Boots of Swiftness. The Orb flew right into Natalie's hand.

"Yep," Natalie said. "Those boots definitely work."

As Garrett landed the ghast, Natalie and Dawn ran to hug him and Henry. "Garrett," Natalie said, "I never thought I'd say this, but I'm glad you're alive."

Starting to zombify, Malgosha let out a terrible wail. The remaining piglins fled for the Nether portal as it closed forever.

Steve held his diamond blade to Malgosha's throat. "You've failed, witch," he told her. "The Overworld lives on."

"You too have fallen for the great lie," she managed to growl. "You'll never be happy. Deep down you know that to dream, to hope, to create is to *suffer*. It's what led you to my clutches in the first place."

"You're right," Steve said. "It *is* harder to create things than destroy them. That's why cowards tend to choose the path of destruction. It's easier." He saw that the sunlight had nearly zombified the sorceress completely. "Later, Goshe. Every minute of knowing you has been truly awful."

"One last thing," Malgosha groaned. "Come closer. . . ."

Steve wrinkled his brow, thinking. "Do you have another little knife that you're gonna stab me with?"

"No, no, no," Malgosha wheezed. "I am too weak. Just come closer."

Steve drew closer. Malgosha pulled out another little knife and tried to stab him. But she was too weak. He took the knife away.

"Come on," Steve said, annoyed.

"Worth a shot," Malgosha croaked. "But I will say this one final thing. Simply lean down close. It's a secret."

"No way," Steve said, shaking his head. "Not gonna happen."

"No, it's about *you*," she whispered. "Trust me. Come on down."

Steve leaned down. With a dagger hidden in her

other hand, Malgosha tried to stab him. He easily slapped the knife away.

"You truly are the worst," Steve told her. "Goodbye."

"Okay, okay," Malgosha gasped. "This is it! Come back. I have no more knives. Where would I even keep one?"

Steve walked away. Malgosha, almost totally a zombie, pulled a knife from a sheath strapped to her ankle and threw it at him. But she was so weak, the blade only traveled two feet and clattered to the ground.

With that, Malgosha breathed her last foul, stinky breath, to be mourned by no one.

CHAPTER TWENTY-SIX

Henry, Natalie, Dawn, and Garrett stood outside the portal leading back to Earth. Steve held the combined Orb and Earth Crystal box, which would open the portal. Midport villagers gathered to watch the visitors who had saved their world depart. The map seller stepped forward, bowed, and handed Natalie a rolled-up map.

"A little late, but thank you," she said, taking the map.

"The real world." Steve sighed. "Are you sure you want to go back there, Henry? It won't feel like this." He gestured at the beautiful land around them, the Overworld. "In the real world you've got judgments, constraints, obstacles."

"I know," Henry said, shrugging. "I'm gonna go make stuff anyway."

Grinning widely, Steve said, "I like that. You're a brave kid."

Prouder than ever of her little brother, Natalie mussed his hair.

Steve knelt by Dennis, who spoke to him in soft barks and yips.

"Of course I love you," Steve answered. "That's why I think this is a good idea. I just got out of piggy prison, so I'm gonna be knocking around for a bit. I'll look for some part-time work, something I can do with my hands." He nodded toward Dawn. "You deserve a home, Dennis. A lawn. And I know she can give you as much love as me."

Dennis licked Steve's face lovingly.

Dawn stepped closer to the pair of pals. "Steve, are you sure about this?"

"I am," Steve said. "He changed my life. It's time for him to change yours. Your bond with Dennis is strong. When he looks at you, it's almost like he's spraying little hearts."

Steve and Dawn hugged. "Thank you, Steve," she said. "Truly."

As Dawn and Dennis stepped through the portal, Steve sang a song to Dennis about how he was the wolf of Steve's dreams but now it was time to change Dawn's life.

"Goodbye, Garrett," Steve said. "You are a truly bodacious warrior—and a good friend."

"Goodbye, Steve. I wish you'd come home with us," Garrett said, clasping his hand. "Hank's cool, but I don't really have any friends my age. We'd make a great team. Vaya con díos. That means 'goodbye, brother.'"

"No it doesn't," Natalie pointed out.

"It sure does," Garrett insisted.

Garrett stepped through the portal. Henry watched him go. Then he approached the portal, stopped, and took a deep breath. He looked back at Natalie and realized she was hesitating.

"Ready?" he asked her.

She took a final look at the gleaming expanse of the Overworld. The sun danced off its mountains and glens. Its colors seemed more vibrant than ever. "Yeah," she said. "I'm gonna miss this place."

Natalie put her arm around Henry's shoulder, and they stepped through the portal together.

Steve stood there a moment, staring at the portal. Then he said, "Oh, to heck with it. I'm coming, too," and jumped through!

Back home in Chuglass, Idaho, all five adventurers found new success, inspired by their experiences in the Overworld.

With Dennis as her main attraction, Dawn had all the petting zoo customers she could handle. She was able to let all her other side businesses go and concentrate on being a full-time zookeeper.

Garrett's Game Over World became the most popular store in town. Showing a new generation the power of games to bring players together gave him great joy. He especially loved sharing the video game he'd designed with Henry. Inspired by their adventures in the Overworld, it was a new game that could be played on a classic arcade cabinet. Natalie painted an awesome scene on the side of the cabinet, filled with images from the Overworld. Players loved it!

Steve often performed at the store, singing for enthusiastic fans. More than once, dance parties broke out!

Natalie finally finished unpacking boxes and putting the house in order the way she and Henry liked it. The last box she opened was labeled NAT'S STUFF. Digging down to the bottom, she found a blank sketchbook just like Henry's. On the back page, her mom had written *TO NATALIE. DREAM AWAY. LOVE, MOM.*

Smiling, Natalie reached for a paintbrush and started to draw. She didn't even care whether her painting was any good or not. She just wanted to create something. Something new. Something no one had ever seen before.

Henry had inspired her!

ABOUT THE AUTHOR

David Lewman is a children's book author who has written more than 150 books based on beloved franchises such as the DC Super Heroes, SpongeBob SquarePants, Jurassic World, Trolls, and many other popular characters. He wrote the original novel *Before the Batman* based on the film *The Batman,* and he's currently at work on an original Superman novel based on the upcoming film *Superman Legacy.* He has also written for television and comics. David lives in Los Angeles with his wife, Donna, and their dog, Gomby.

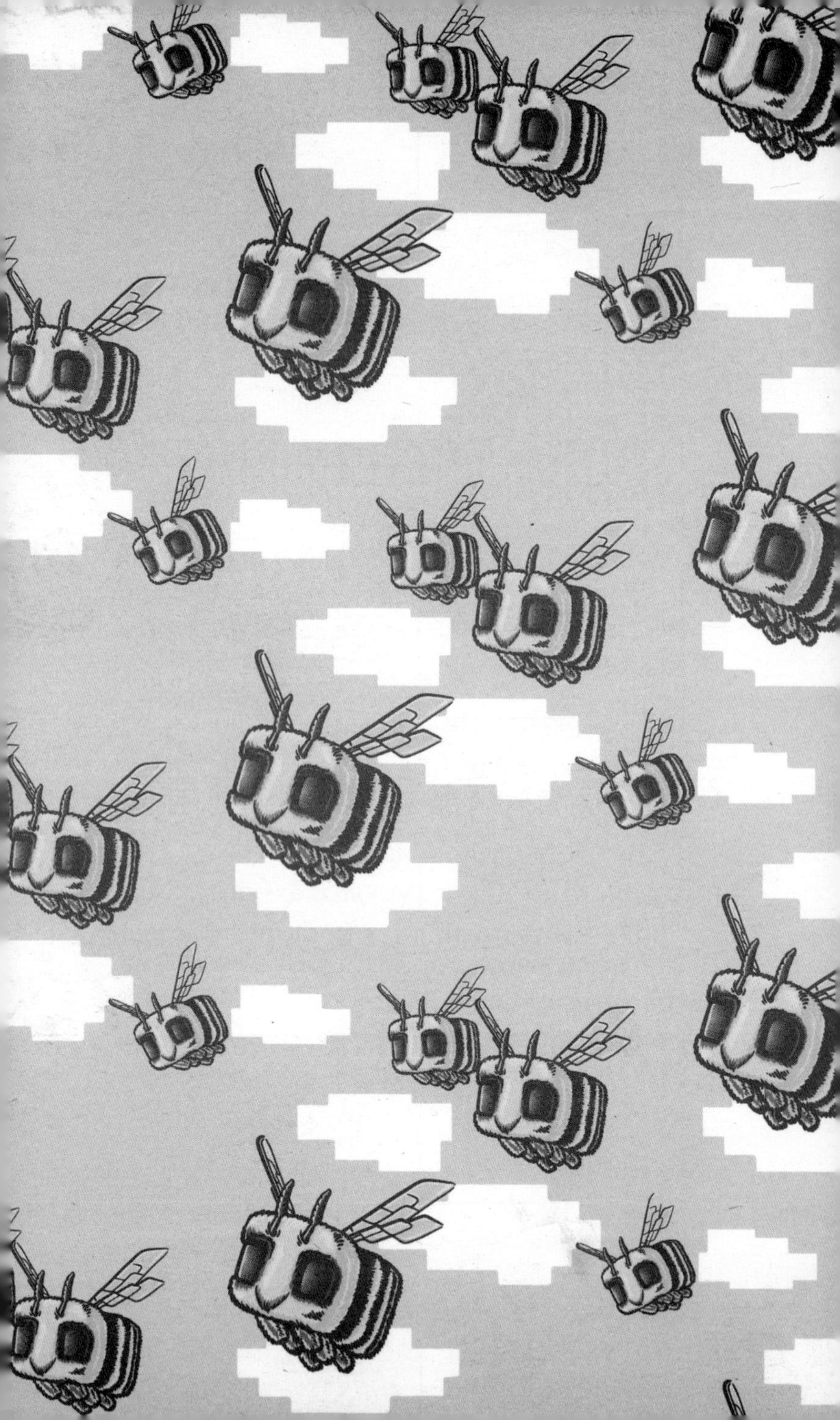